The North Atlantic Coast

The *Stories from Where We Live* Series

Each volume in the *Stories from Where We Live* series celebrates a North American ecoregion through its own distinctive literature. For thousands of years, people have told stories to convey their community's cultural and natural history. *Stories from Where We Live* reinvigorates that tradition in hopes of helping young people better understand the place where they live. The anthologies feature poems, stories, and essays from historical and contemporary authors as well as from the oral traditions of each region's indigenous peoples. Together they document the geographic richness of the continent and reflect the myriad ways that people interact with and respond to the natural world. We hope that these stories kindle readers' imaginations and inspire them to explore, observe, ponder, and protect the place they call home.

Please visit www.milkweed.org/worldashome for a teaching guide to this book and more information on the *Stories from Where We Live* series.

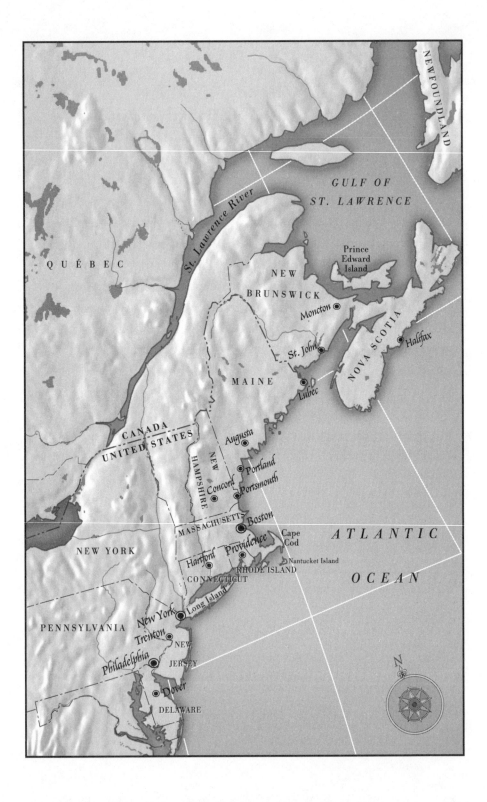

The North Atlantic Coast

Stories from Where We Live

Edited by Sara St. Antoine

Maps by Paul Mirocha
Illustrations by Trudy Nicholson

MILKWEED EDITIONS

Published 2000 by Milkweed Editions
Printed in Canada
Illustrations by Trudy Nicholson
Maps by Paul Mirocha
Interior design by Wendy Holdman
The text of this book is set in Legacy.
04   05   06   07   08   5   4   3   2   1
First Paperback Edition

Milkweed Editions, a nonprofit publisher,
specially thanks Joe B. and Harriet Foster for their
generous underwriting support of this book.

Milkweed also gratefully acknowledges support from Emilie and Henry Buchwald; Bush Foundation; Cargill Incorporated; Timothy and Tara Clark Family Charitable Fund; DeL Corazón Family Fund; Dougherty Family Foundation; Ecolab Foundation; Joe B. Foster Family Foundation; General Mills Foundation; Jerome Foundation; Kathleen Jones; Constance B. Kunin; D. K. Light; Chris and Ann Malecek; McKnight Foundation; a grant from the Minnesota State Arts Board, through an appropriation by the Minnesota State Legislature, a grant from the National Endowment for the Arts, and private funders; Sheila C. Morgan; Laura Jane Musser Fund; an award from the National Endowment for the Arts, which believes that a great nation deserves great art; Navarre Corporation; Kate and Stuart Nielsen; Outagamie Charitable Foundation; Qwest Foundation; Debbie Reynolds; St. Paul Companies, Inc., Foundation; Ellen and Sheldon Sturgis; Surdna Foundation; Target, Marshall Field's, and Mervyn's with support from the Target Foundation; Gertrude Sexton Thompson Charitable Trust (George R.A. Johnson, Trustee); James R. Thorpe Foundation; Toro Foundation; Weyerhaeuser Family Foundation; and Xcel Energy Foundation.

Library of Congress Cataloging-in-Publication Data

The North Atlantic coast / edited by Sara St. Antoine ; maps by Paul Mirocha ; illustrations by Trudy Nicholson.— 1st ed.
        p. cm. — (Stories from where we live)
Includes index.
ISBN 1-57131-643-4 (pbk. : alk. paper)
        1. Atlantic Coast (New England)—Miscellanea—Juvenile lieterature. 2. Atlantic Coast (Middle Atlantic States)—Miscellanea—Juvenile literature. 3. Atlantic Coast (Canada)—Miscellanea—Juvenile literature. 4. Natural history—Atlantic Coast (New England)—Miscellanea—Juvenile literature. 5. Natural history—Atlantic Coast (Middle Atlantic States)—Miscellanea—Juvenile literature. 6. Natural history—Atlantic Coast (Canada)—Miscellanea—Juvenile literature. I. St. Antoine, Sara, 1966- II. Series.

F12.A74N665 2000
975—dc22

                                                                                    2004003600

This book is printed on acid-free paper.

The North Atlantic Coast

Reapers and Sowers

Wild Lives

Appendixes: Ecology of the North Atlantic Coast

An Invitation

Have you ever held a shell to your ear and listened to its roar? No matter where you are, that sound can be enough to transport you to the edge of the sea—where the wind whistles and the waves crash.

We hope that this book will be a bit like that seashell. Pick it up and listen to what each of these authors has to say about life along the North Atlantic Coast. Maybe you'll start to feel like you're standing on the seashore. Or bobbing along on a lobster boat. Or watching snails shimmy up a stalk of marsh grass.

As the stories, essays, poems, and journals in this anthology make clear, the communities that line the coast from Newfoundland to Delaware are varied, life-filled places. They include tiny fishing villages, farming communities, college towns, and some of North America's biggest cities—including Boston and New York City. They comprise inlets, estuaries, city parks, mud flats, salt marshes, backyards, and barrier beaches. At the same time, these communities have a common bond in their proximity to the great Atlantic Ocean.

Stories from Where We Live—The North Atlantic Coast portrays this ecological region through the literature that is its alone. You probably know that people have been sharing stories about the place where they live for thousands of years. Maybe you've heard a local legend from long ago, or listened to your grandparents tell stories about your town from the days when they were young. We believe these stories are the key to helping us better understand—and appreciate—the world around us.

Stories help us recall the history of our communities and see the ways they have changed over time. They teach us about other people who live there. They remind us of the creatures that dive, fly, creep, and scuttle around us. They entice us to become explorers! And, in many cases, they inspire us to become caretakers of all that is wild and wonderful in our home community.

With that in mind, we've collected some of the stories of people who have inhabited the North Atlantic Coast over the centuries, from early Wampanoag Indians to eighteenth-century seafarers to contemporary teens. As you'll see, we've divided the anthology into four parts: "Adventures" recounts both lighthearted and thrilling moments of action and exploration along the Atlantic; "Great Places" brings to life some favorite wild sites; "Reapers and Sowers" shows ways that local people have drawn sustenance from—and nurtured—the natural world around them; and "Wild Lives" portrays the creatures making a home on land or at sea.

We hope you enjoy this homegrown literary collection. And whether you live along the Atlantic coast or are merely stopping in for an armchair visit, we hope you'll discover some of the reasons it's a fascinating and beloved place.

—Sara St. Antoine

The North Atlantic Coast

Adventures

Sail by the Moon

GRETCHEN WOELFLE

Iceboats have long been used for recreation on lakes and rivers where the ice freezes thick. This story takes place in the late 1800s. Today you can find enthusiastic iceboaters from Maine to Washington State—and in Canada and Europe, too.

On Chester Erskine's eleventh birthday, his father said, "It's time to build you an iceboat. I did it and so did your grandfather, and his father too."

"Will I have to sail her alone?" Chester asked.

"A-yuh," Father answered. "Maine boys do that."

Chester frowned. "Why wasn't I born in Boston?"

"You've got nothing to worry about, son," Father chuckled.

Every winter the two of them sailed from their farm at the head of Damariscotta Lake down toward the Narrows, where the lake fell into a river that ran to the sea. The iceboat whizzed faster than the wind that stung Chester's eyes and froze his cheeks. The blades scratched the ice and hissed past beaver lodges covered in snow. The beavers stayed warm inside. Chester kept warm sitting close to Father.

Over the years Father had guided Chester's hand in steering clear of jagged ice that could flip a boat. He showed Chester how to let out the sail and lean to the side when the wind tipped the boat on two runners. Father's gentle hand corrected all his mistakes.

Chester loved to sail in light breezes, but when a strong northwest wind blew, he gave Father the tiller. What if a big wind came up when he was sailing alone?

I'll be a year a-building, Chester thought. I won't think about it now.

Chester and Father cut pine trees in February. All spring they sawed and planed the planks. They made a frame for the boat in the shape of a cross, and strengthened it with two braces.

"Back in 1871 when I was a boy," declared Father, "an iceboat won a race against the New York-Chicago express train."

"Will mine go that fast?" asked Chester.

"Not quite," Father said. "Maybe as fast as the local train to Portland."

That's still too fast, Chester thought.

During the summer Chester nailed slats across the boat to make a platform. Then he sanded the wood as smooth as the lake in early morning. The summer sun raised a sweet smell from the sawdust. Winter seemed far away.

When maple leaves turned red and yellow, Chester filed three steel runners until they gleamed. Father helped him bolt one runner on each side, and one on a swivel in the back.

"She'll turn on a dime," Father said.

Chester wasn't sure he wanted to turn that fast. He knew what it took to turn a boat—minding the sail, steering just right, and keeping all three runners on the ice.

By the first snow, he had attached a tiller and sanded the mast.

"Are you ready to take her out?" Mother asked as they sewed the canvas sail.

"I suppose so," Chester mumbled.

"I remember when your father was tending a sickly calf and you drove the hay wagon to the barn, just in time to beat a thunderstorm. You didn't think you could handle the horses, but you did."

"Those horses just plodded through the field," protested Chester. "They didn't run as fast as a railroad train!"

"You've got a steady hand," replied Mother. "You'll do just fine."

One bright day in January their neighbor, Mr. Bond, came to visit. "They say the lake is frozen all the way across," he reported.

"Tomorrow you can launch your boat, son," Father said.

"Maybe I should walk across the lake to check the ice," Chester offered.

"Linwood Brewer's done it," said Mr. Bond. "He's the one that told me."

I would have found some thin ice, Chester thought.

Father and Mr. Bond helped Chester carry the iceboat from the barn to the lake. "She's ready to go," said Father.

"Don't you want to come along?" Chester asked him.

"No, she's all yours." Father clapped him on the shoulder.

Father and Mr. Bond played checkers while Chester set the table for midday dinner.

Mr. Bond ate two helpings of everything, including Mother's apple pie, still warm from the oven.

"Chester," said Father, "if you take Mr. Bond home in your iceboat, we can play checkers all afternoon."

Chester's apple pie sank in his stomach. How could he refuse? Mr. Bond lived directly across the lake, a three-mile walk on an icy road.

"I'll go if you're willing, Mr. Bond," Chester said.

"I grew up by the ocean and never sailed an iceboat," he replied.

"You'll make good ballast after this meal," Father said.

Everyone laughed but Chester. After dinner he walked down to the boat. He ran his hand over the smooth planks. The wind was light, and Mr. Bond was heavy. Things might go all right.

When Mr. Bond finally jumped Father's last king, he exclaimed, "This is my lucky day. I'll celebrate on Chester's iceboat!"

Chester wrapped a scarf around his neck and tucked the ends under his collar. He strapped spikes to his boots. Mr. Bond pulled a woolen cap over his bald head. Mother and Father came to see them off. The long afternoon shadows reached across the snow and down to the lake.

Chester walked out on the ice. It was so smooth and clear he could see his shadow in the mud below. Black ice, he thought, the fastest ice of the winter.

"You're sure Chester can sail alone?" asked Mr. Bond, getting on the boat.

Mother laughed. "Of course he can!"

"He's been practicing since he was six," Father added. "But mind the ice slabs, son. They can be dangerous."

Chester wanted to run away—to the house, to the barn, to the woods. Instead he shouted, "Here we go!" and pushed the boat onto the frozen lake, his spikes crunching as he ran. He leaped aboard and pulled in the sail.

Mr. Bond clutched the side as the boat shot forward. "Waaait . . ." His voice faded in the wind.

Chester strained to see ahead. He saw jagged ice and clutched the tiller, pushing it just an inch. The boat lurched to the right, skittish as a high-strung horse. As they bumped over the jagged ice, Chester realized he'd pushed the tiller the wrong way.

"Stupid mistake!" hissed Chester.

"Slooow dooown!" moaned Mr. Bond.

Chester pulled in the sail and the boat went faster. "Wrong again," he muttered. He let out the sail and the boat slowed.

He had to change course to get to Mr. Bond's house. "Coming about! Duck, Mr. Bond!"

This time he turned the tiller and worked the sail just right. He smiled at Mr. Bond, but his neighbor stared hard at the ice, his lips pressed tightly together.

He's more nervous than I am! Chester thought. He tried to chuckle but coughed instead. Cold wind stung his throat.

Ahead the ice had buckled and thrown big slabs up three, four, five feet high. His heart pounded. What would Father do? Chester sailed along the ice wall until he spied an opening.

"Coming about! Hold on!" he shouted. A side runner rose off the ice as the boat sailed through. Chips of ice stung their cheeks.

"Stop!" gasped Mr. Bond.

"Lean!" shouted Chester. Mr. Bond sat frozen. "Lean!" Chester shouted again. He pushed against Mr. Bond and the runner returned to the ice. The land rushed toward them.

"My house!" Mr. Bond pointed.

Chester let out the sail and dragged his spikes on the ice till the boat stopped. Mr. Bond stood up, his knees shaking.

"Thank you, Chester," he said. "It was a once in a lifetime experience . . . for me anyway."

Chester waved and pushed off again. The boat was lighter now, and faster. Daylight was nearly gone. He hunched his shoulders and peered around the sail.

He glided through the opening in the slabs of ice. Suddenly a gust of wind caught the back runner and lifted it off the ice. The boat began to spin. Chester's scarf flew across his eyes and disappeared. He grabbed the sides as the boat whirled round and round, the sail flapping angrily. Chester waited for the crash against the slabs and the jolt that would fling him out onto the ice.

What if the boat smashed to pieces? What if he broke his leg? Would he freeze to death on the lake?

Without thinking, Chester leaned back. He felt the back runner touch the ice. The boat kept spinning. He stretched his legs until his spikes gripped the ice and the boat slowed. Finally it stopped. He lay on his back and looked at the deep blue sky. He and Father had never had a boat flicker like this. But he'd done the right thing and saved the boat and himself from harm.

Chester walked back to find his scarf. As he wound it round his neck, he gazed at his boat. She was a beauty and he could sail her alone.

The wind filled the sails and he took off down the lake. For the first time, he saw the full moon shining bright. Ice mounds sparkled like heaps of diamonds.

Why go home yet? He could sail by the moon. The wind lifted a side runner. The boat leaped ahead. Chester clutched the tiller, then relaxed. He balanced the boat so the runner stayed a foot off the ice. He was floating, he was flying.

I could beat an express train! he thought.

Snow-clad pine trees glowed along the shore. The wind whistled in his ears. The runners scraped white across the black ice as Chester circled a small island. He passed a snowy mound and called, "Hello, beavers!"

He raced up the lake. "Faster," he called to the wind and laughed out loud in the frosty air. The moon lit up a path to lead him home.

⌄⌄

Gretchen Woelfle *writes children's stories and environmental nonfiction in Venice, California. Her grandfather-in-law, Chester Erskine, was born in 1881 on a farm in Jefferson, Maine, on the shores of Damariscotta Lake. He grew up to be the fastest iceboater on the lake. He married Iva McArdle in 1907, and they moved to Connecticut. In 1939 they bought a small cottage on the lake, not far from the old Erskine farm. They spent every summer there till they died in 1967. Chester and Iva's sons, grandchildren, and great-grandchildren continue to visit the cottage each year. Chester's iceboat is long gone, but the Erskines still swim and sail on Damariscotta Lake during the summer.*

The Rescuer from Lime Rock

STEPHEN CURRIE

Lime Rock is a tiny island off the Newport coast that is now called Ida Lewis Rock in honor of its famous lighthouse keeper. Although the original tower light was officially discontinued in 1927, the light attached to the keeper's house is kept lit as an ongoing tribute to Ida Lewis.

Huge waves crashed against the shore. A cold wind raced across the ocean, sending spray everywhere. Rain mixed with snow and ice pelted down. If you had been in Newport, Rhode Island, on that March day back in 1869, you might have enjoyed the violent storm—from indoors!

On Lime Rock, a small island near Newport, Ida Lewis had been sneezing and coughing all afternoon. Ida was a lighthouse keeper. Each night she lit the huge lamp that guided ships safely into Newport Harbor. She had just propped her chilly bare feet next to the kitchen oven when she heard a cry. Ida knew what it meant: out on the ocean, a boat had tipped over.

Ida didn't hesitate. "I started right out, just as I was," she recalled years later: no shoes, no jacket, no hat. Ignoring her mother, who begged her to stay inside, Ida ran to the rowboat she kept on the beach. Far from shore, two men were struggling in the icy water. Could she reach them in time?

Quickly Ida slid her boat into the waves and began to row. It was hard work. The wind made steering almost impossible, and waves splashed over her every few seconds. Luckily Ida was strong and determined, and she never lost sight of her target. Little by little she worked her way through the storm toward the drowning men.

But getting there was only part of the problem. Bringing the men into the boat would be just as hard. Ida knew they would not be able to help themselves. First she stroked hard on one oar, turning the boat so its broad stern faced the struggling men. Then she braced her legs against the side of the boat and reached into the black, frigid water.

She had steered well. One of the men, nearly unconscious, was within reach. Seizing his hand, she turned him onto his back and pulled him toward her. Then she reached under his shoulders and locked her arms securely around his chest.

Ida balanced as steadily as she could in the rocking surf. With all her might, she heaved the man up and back. She pulled again, drawing more of his body over the side, but it took several lifts before his knees cleared the stern. Ida made sure he was still breathing. Then, leaving him at the bottom of the boat, she fished the other man out of the water, too.

Even now, the rescue was not over. Between the boat and safety lay a hundred yards of wind and waves. Shivering with cold, her strength almost gone, Ida rowed through the blinding spray. Again, her aim was perfect. One last pull on the oars, and she was safely on the beach. Ida had saved the men from certain drowning. Now she *really* had a reason to warm her feet.

Lime Rock saw plenty of boating accidents. Some people forgot to watch for rocks, and others went out when the wind and waves were too strong. Still others couldn't handle a boat properly. But few of the accident victims drowned. During fifty years of keeping the Lime Rock lighthouse, Ida single-handedly rescued seventeen people—and most of the other rescues were just as dangerous as this one.

In 1866, for instance, a soldier overturned his boat on a windy February night. Luckily Ida knew the harbor well. Using the lighthouse beam to guide her, Ida steered around jagged rocks and up to the struggling solider, then rowed him to safety.

Another winter, three farmers set off across the harbor in a leaky boat, trying to catch an escaped sheep that was swimming toward the ocean. When they capsized, Ida rowed out, pulled all three farmers into her own boat, and brought them to shore. Then she went back to save the sheep!

But Ida's bravest rescue of all didn't involve her boat. In 1881 two men who were walking across the frozen harbor fell through a patch of thin ice. Fortunately, Ida saw them from Lime Rock. She had to run a half mile across the treacherous ice and pull both of them out of the chilly water. She said many years later, "I never thought of danger when people needed help."

Living on a tiny island had taught Ida to be resourceful and independent. She had many jobs, from polishing the beacon lights to doing the laundry. She rowed her sister and brothers to school in Newport each morning and rowed back to pick them up every afternoon. And Ida had learned early on to do whatever had to be done. Her father had been Lime Rock's lighthouse keeper before her, but when he had a stroke and could no longer work, she took over. Not everyone approved. A few people felt that being a lighthouse keeper was unladylike, and some said that women were too weak to do the job properly—even while Ida was busy rescuing one person after another!

But Ida never cared what other people thought, nor did she believe that she was unusually brave. Although her rescues made her famous, she disliked the attention. "If there were some people out there who needed help," she told a writer, "I would get into my boat and go to them even if I knew I couldn't get back. Wouldn't you?" Like taking over for her father or rowing to Newport every school day, rescuing people was something that simply had to be done. "I just went," she said, "and that was all there was to it."

Stephen Currie *is the author of about forty books and many magazine articles. He lives with his family in upstate New York.*

The Ocean Is a Heartbeat

MARY QUIGLEY

The ocean is a heartbeat.
Within circulates me,
a dolphin.
Seeing sound,
I split the waves in two,
quietly,
like
a lullaby.

A lullaby
is a heartbeat
for me,
a child.
Ocean music playing
from a shell
pressed upon my ear
as

I drift
on waves.

I drift,

to sleep.

Waves change,
a crashing pulse upon the shore.
The air feels different,

storm is coming.

Storm is coming.
Wake up!
Oatmeal and juice.
We need more food.
To the market for
bottled water,
peanut butter,
canned soup.
Don't forget
crackers and

Eat more
tuna fish.

tuna fish.

Catch twice as many tuna fish.
Must be ready to swim far,
dive deep,
do without,
and make it through the storm.
Mother nudges at my side,
helps me catch fish.
Water churns.

Wind churns.
Land,

water

merge,

foam.

Better go farther,

Better go farther,

deeper,

into

the ocean.

Below the churning waves
and flying debris
I hold my breath longer.
Lunging through the mix of
air and water,
I blast with
my blowhole,
clearing away the spray
to make way for a quick,
deep
breath.
Hold my breath.

away from
the ocean.

Hold my breath.
I hope the lights
don't go out as they
flicker.
Radio crackles and
fails.
Light candles.
Study map.
Mama and Papa pack and
we drive west,
beyond the waves
and flying debris.

Only to return again.

Only to return again.

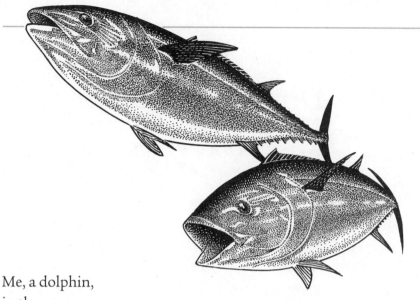

Me, a dolphin,
in the ocean,

Me, a child, on the
shore.

when the ocean is a heartbeat,
steady, pulsing.
And
Mama helps me catch
a fish.

Mama helps me catch
a fish.

Mary Quigley *is a wife, mother, and author with experience in teaching and nature study. She has supervised a program for academically at-risk youth and taught history to college students. She is frequently found enjoying a garden, museum, pond, or bookstore.*

Dorchester Days

ALICE STONE BLACKWELL

As a child, Alice Stone Blackwell lived with her parents on a high hill in Dorchester, Massachusetts, overlooking Boston to the north and the Atlantic Ocean to the east. Her parents were both suffragists, and her mother ran a newspaper devoted to women's issues. Alice's days were enlivened by her parents' activities and by the opportunities for adventure and play in the gardens, woods, and water near her home. She began the journal excerpted below in 1872 when she was fourteen years old.

March 20th

Wednesday. A strange and wonderful day; a mixture of clouds, sunshine, cold, and a wind that made the elms bend and crack, roared around the schoolhouse, made us all wild at recess, and blew me home after school in a wild whirl of skirts, coat, cloud, hair, hat and dust. Made tart crusts. Emma arrived under convoy of Mama, and was fed and seen to. She immediately set to work clipping slips for the *Journal* like a born editor.

April 26th

Friday. Awfully and outrageously hot. I could have Oh'ed for a lodge in a garden of cucumbers, for the first time this year. I went up with Miss Tucker to the house, did a wee bit of gardening and dug up part of the patch for my beans. There was a big wind toward evening, whirling weird white clouds of dust along the road, and Annie and I went out and got blown.

July 6th

Saturday. Had a beautiful sail with Mr. and Mrs. Campbell. They were to hoist a black flag, and I was put upon the watch for it, and wished it had been my pirate lover. When it appeared Papa, Mama, Mrs. Dennet and I drove down to the shore in the carriage, and found Mrs. C. sitting in the boat, her husband having gone up to the house to call us. When he came back we had a beautiful sail, lunching on cake and crackers, and landed on Moon island,* where we stayed just long enough for me to take a delightful bath. Moon Isl. reminds me of M[artha's] V[ineyard] only the cliffs are not high enough, and are grass grown. We landed at Squantum, where the carriage awaited us, and drove home with Mrs. Campbell.
Moon Island is now a peninsular extension of Squantum.

Sept. 20th

Friday. Clouds wind and sunshine. After school walked over to some beautiful woods in the direction of Milton, and got a lot of moss, partridge vines and sweet acorns.

Oct. 4th

Friday. Had the fullest intention of going Miltonward, but Emma Adams asked me to go out rowing, and I accepted with pleasure of course. Hattie went with us, and we all three raced to Commercial point. The boat was launched with some trouble, and we started out. It was delightful to be on blue water once more, and be able to dip my hand in the blessed brine. We had to come back at last, and I had leave to row one oar, which I liked. Hattie and Emma gave me contradictory orders, but I obeyed the Skipper of course. As we made for the pier, we ran aground in the mud. I pushed the boat off once, but it stuck again—fast. And the tide was still falling. And rowing, and pushing, and laughter and vexation, were of no use; we couldn't stir her a hair's breadth. A little crowd of men and boys collected on the wharf and watched us with great amusement. A man hailed us from one of the little vessels at anchor, and bawled to us to push off and row so and so. He might as well have told us to go to the moon; we *couldn't* push off; that was just it. Finally he came to our assistance in a wherry, took Hattie and me into his boat, and towing and pushing and tugging and grunting hauled our boat into the channel; paddled after an oar we had left stuck in the mud, received our thanks and paddled away. We only ran aground once more, and were triumphantly hauled up to the pier by a rope we flung to the men and boys thereon collected. We then retreated to a boathouse and exploded.

April 12th
Saturday. Went in to the dentist, and came out with Mamma through a heavy snowstorm. Mr. & Mrs. Horne and baby were on the platform, & Mamma offered to drive the two last up when our carriage came. Mr. H. said he would go on home and light the fire, and overtook me, I having started to walk up. We went on together, and the snowflakes were huge, as big as birds.

April 20th
Sunday. Went over to Chapel, walking with Fanny, whom I overtook. It was not as nice as in the afternoon, and there were

few there. Rode over to Quincy Great Hill or Head with the folks. It is a glorious place—a great round hill with water all around it, and great cliffs that seemed almost like Martha's Vineyard. I watched my face in the blessed salt water, and heard the sound of it; but it was nearly spoiled by Edith's incessant noise and chatter, which gave me a headache.

May 14th

Wednesday. Went to music lesson. Cut dandelion greens in the evening with Miss Jones and Edie. Got letters from Kitty and Aunt Marian. Went out walking after supper with Edie, and walked a mile and a half in 30^{m}.

June 4th

Wednesday. Sent in a huge bunch of lilies of the valley to be divided among the girls in the printing office. I think it is such a pity the flowers should all be in one place and the people in another! We have more flowers than we know what to do with. Edie's last day here. She sent her goodbye to Miss Morse by me. Played croquet with her, and let her beat the last game, it being the last.

June 8th

Sunday. Rode over to the Quincy granite quarries with Papa and Mamma, and he & I climbed up to the top, saw the view and got 5 leaved ivy & ferns, also Solomon's seal & I an armfull of ~~colubines~~ wake robin—one huge specimen nearly half as long again as my arm, measuring from root to leaf tip. It is a lovely romantic place & I mean to go again.

July 28th

Monday. Flo arrived. I saw the queerest fog bank coming in from sea when I was on the house top watching. Went shopping in Boston with Mamma. We mutually begged each other to put on our tombstones

"Died of shopping with an unreasonable mother"

"Died of shopping with an impracticable daughter."

Alice Stone Blackwell *was the daughter of suffragists Lucy Stone and Henry Blackwell. She grew up to be a social reformer, writer, and editor.*

The Legend of Big Claw

JEFF W. BENS

for my father, David L. Bens, a great teller of stories

Block Island, where this story takes place, is known as "the island of hope" because so many of its remarkable natural areas—high cliffs, dunes, moorlands, salt ponds, marshes, beaches, and more—have been protected through the actions of its loyal residents.

Luther stood by the lobster traps at the Old Harbor docks, watching a ferry boat crossing from the mainland. His father had been captain of that boat, ferrying passengers from Point Judith, Rhode Island, out to Block Island and back again, every hour on the hour during the summer. A crowd of people lined the dock waiting for the ferry to land. Block Island was a funny place: for three seasons Luther could bike all over the island and hardly see anyone he didn't know, or hardly anyone period, but in the summer the island was packed with people from the mainland.

"Swarmed," with people, his Uncle Bill would say.

Jenny Swanson was from the mainland. Luther didn't think a lot about Jenny Swanson, but when he did his head went hot and his stomach felt like it would if he were falling off a cliff. He'd seen her only once. She had blonde hair and brown eyes and she wore a t-shirt for a rock band that neither Luther, nor the guy who ran the Block Island Music Shoppe, had ever heard of.

Jenny Swanson's family was renting Uncle Bill's house for the summer, and that's how Luther had met her. He and his little sister, Kate, had been biking along the road that went past the Mohegan Bluffs when Luther felt the air go out of his tire. Luther had a patch kit and a pump at home, but home was on the other side of the island, overlooking Great Salt Pond. So he and Kate went by his uncle's house to see if there was a pump in the garage. Jenny Swanson answered the door. She was pulling a green elastic from the ponytail in her hair. Her hair fell across her shoulders.

"My tire broke," Luther said. He felt his face go red.

Jenny Swanson laughed. Luther couldn't look at her. Kate got the pump and caught up with him. He was practically running his bicycle down the road.

"Hey, Captain!"

It was Uncle Bill, with a bait bucket in each hand.

"You look like you've seen a ghost," Uncle Bill said. Bill was wearing denim cutoff shorts and a hat that said "What's Cookin'?"

"I was just thinking," Luther said.

Uncle Bill's boat, named *Cathy's Cloud*, was a small one compared to the big boats that fished traps farther out to sea. Those boats were sometimes forty feet long and had diesel engines and depth sounders and radar and fished hundreds of traps. Bill's boat had a gasoline engine and a leaky place in the deck, and Luther could walk from bow to stern in ten paces.

His uncle didn't work a lot of lobster traps, but in August and early September he brought in enough lobster to pay Luther five dollars for a morning's help. His uncle let Luther tend a couple of traps. Luther had marked them with a green shamrock, because his family was Irish-American and because he loved the Boston Celtics.

They loaded up the boat and pushed back from the slip. Luther took a big breath and exhaled up toward the sun. He liked the way the ocean smelled, especially when he was out in the middle of it, not just lying on some beach. When they'd cleared the harbor, Uncle Bill let Luther take the wheel. Luther kept the course set from the compass. He knew how to read navigational maps if he ever needed to. His father had shown him.

They passed the Point Judith ferry as it neared the harbor, and Luther could see the passengers out on the deck—whole families in sunglasses throwing bread crumbs to hovering gulls. He'd ridden sometimes in the bridge of that ferry with his father. His father had died of cancer when Luther was seven, four years ago. In the end his father couldn't leave his own bed, though this is not the way Luther wanted to remember him.

Uncle Bill put a hand on Luther's shoulder. Luther relaxed his grip on the wheel.

"Maybe my new hauler will finally haul in old Big Claw." Uncle Bill raised his eyebrows a couple of times and pulled on his gloves. The hauler was a hydraulic pulley that lifted the traps from the ocean floor. Uncle Bill used to haul the traps up with his hands.

"Big Claw's got to be ten feet long by now," Luther said. He smiled a little. "You'd need bigger traps."

Uncle Bill laughed. Big Claw was famous among the lobster-men on the island. He was sort of like Block Island's own Loch Ness monster.

Luther's father had told Big Claw stories when Luther was little. They'd sit with his mother and Kate on the screen porch, looking out across Great Salt Pond. As the sun sank into the Atlantic, his father would light his pipe, and Luther would have a lemonade, and Kate would be hanging onto her stuffed horse, and his father would tell them about the time when Big Claw was small.

"When I was just a boy," his father would begin, "the Delancey boys pulled him up in their father's trap. He wasn't much of a lobster then, sort of a runt."

The blue heron, the one that was there every summer, would glide low along Great Salt Pond's shore. Later, when his father was unable to go for walks along the pond, Luther would give him reports on the herons, and the osprey with their gray wings, and the sniggling plovers.

"The Delancey boys were mean kids," his father would continue. "They sometimes liked to set two lobsters on the bait table and have them fight."

Luther's mother would shake her head at this point and smile. She'd heard the stories even more times than Luther.

"Big Claw didn't want to fight, but the Delancey boys made him, pushing him toward a big, mean-looking lobster, who snapped at him with its claws. 'Fight, fight!' the Delancey boys shouted. They poked at Big Claw and snapped him with elastic bands." Here his father would straighten up excitedly beside Luther on the couch, the way he always did when he came to the good part of a story. "The Delancey boys snapped Big Claw one too many times. Suddenly, Big Claw spun around

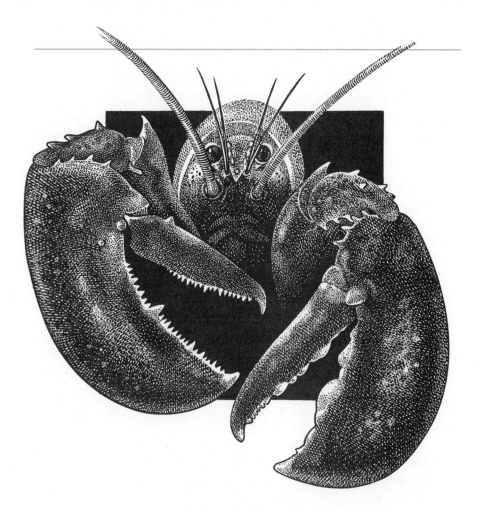

and chomped onto the big brother's thumb, then he swept the other lobster, mean as it was, right back into the water."

"And Big Claw?" Katie would ask, because she hadn't heard the story as often as Luther.

"The Delancey kid leapt to his feet, shook his hand, flung his arm out, 'Yowch!' But Big Claw hung on, until . . ."

Here his father would go quiet, slowly nodding his head, packing his pipe with his thumb.

"Until . . . ," Luther might say, because this part of the story always got to him.

"Until Big Claw made it back to the ocean. But his claw stayed clamped to the Delancey boy's thumb."

There were lots of Big Claw stories, near misses over the years. A few boats even claimed to have had him on board, but somehow Big Claw always managed to get away. Like Big Claw, the stories grew larger over the years. Whenever a trap was snapped from its buoy so the lobstermen couldn't haul it from the bottom of the ocean, it was Big Claw at work. He became the great lobster liberator! And his size! And that big crusher claw! In one story, Big Claw stood ready to signal the U.S. Navy should Axis warships sail into Narragansett Bay. This would have made Big Claw over fifty years old.

You could use just about anything for lobster bait. Uncle Bill used the cheapest fish he could find. Lobsters ate anything: fish, crabs, mussels, starfish, sea urchins, even each other. Luther sometimes felt bad about hauling up lobsters to cook them in a pot. But a person had to eat, and the fact that they sometimes ate each other made him feel like maybe they weren't the nicest creatures. Big Claw was different, though.

Uncle Bill leaned over the side of the boat and hooked the gaff around the first green, white, and orange buoy.

"Would you eat him?" Luther asked.

"Who?"

"Big Claw."

The cork line attached to the buoy was draped with sea kelp. "I'd sure as heck sell him. Fifty pounds at three dollars a pound." Bill hooked the line around his bright hydraulic hauler. "I don't know if I could eat him, though."

The hauler began to spin, slowly pulling the trap up from the bottom of the cove. Uncle Bill stood back and grinned.

"My bad back is smiling." He waved his arms at the water. "Rise, rise!"

There were two lobsters in the kitchen of his trap. They lifted the lobsters out, banded their claws, and measured them. Luther had his own gauge. A lobster couldn't be too small or too big. If it was you had to throw it back. Luther's lobster was a good one, shiny brown and about four pounds. He placed it in the cooler. Uncle Bill's lobster had eggs along the underside of the carapace. Uncle Bill took out his knife, cut a V-shaped notch in the lobster's tail flipper, and dropped her back into the water. The V-notch would let other lobstermen know that the lobster was a female. If you ate all the females, soon there'd be no lobsters left.

"That hauler is going to save my back twenty years of abuse." He looked at Luther. "And you can thank the summer rent from your girlfriend's family for that." Uncle Bill winked at him.

Luther thought, Katie and her big mouth.

Luther sat with his mother and Uncle Bill on the porch overlooking Great Salt Pond. Katie was standing at the water's edge. Luther's dog, Jump Shot, was turning circles and sniffing after fiddler crabs that popped in and out of their muddy holes. The sun sank into the waves.

Luther watched his sister, squawking now like a gull. There weren't a lot of kids on the island, but he had a couple of good friends, and Jump Shot. And when she wasn't acting like a jerk, Katie was OK, too. He'd even given her one of the fishing rods that his father had given him.

Luther and his father had fished the channel for flounder and mackerel. His father had shown him how to cast and troll, how to clean a fish, how to cook it in a frying pan outside over an open flame. Luther missed his father a lot, especially at night on the porch, when the sun was setting behind the cat-tails and the reeds.

His mother looked up from her book. "Uncle Bill and I are going to do a Labor Day clambake," she announced. "We'll need both of your help."

Uncle Bill always did a clambake for someone over Labor Day. There were a lot of ways to make money in the summer on Block Island.

"It's for the Swansons," his mother said. "You know, the doctor's family that rented Bill's house."

Jump Shot yelped. Luther watched a loon dive into the pond.

Luther didn't want to sit on the porch and talk about serv-ing Jenny Swanson quahogs and corn. So he rode the loop, past the Mohegan bluffs where merlins rode warm air cur-rents, effortlessly gliding high above the waves. If you got too close to the edge of the bluffs you were a goner; it was at least a hundred feet to the rocky beach below. Luther wheeled his bike near the edge of the bluff. Wind blew around his already curly hair. He threw a stone as far out as he could. He took a deep breath of ocean air.

In the harbor, a huge crowd gathered outside the Double Dip ice cream shop. Luther rode up to investigate. There must have been fifty people, mostly tourists on mopeds and families he did not recognize. But there were people he did recognize, too, and they seemed very excited. Maybe the Double Dip was giv-ing away free samples. Little kids were up on their fathers' shoulders, laughing and pointing.

Luther saw Captain Murphy. Captain Murphy had one of

the big boats that took the mainlanders out for sea bass and bluefish.

"What's going on in there?" Luther asked.

"Luther! You won't believe it!" It was as if Captain Murphy had just seen Santa Claus come down the Harborview Fish House chimney. "The Johnson boat. In a fish net. They captured Big Claw!"

Luther didn't believe it. But seeing the excited crowd and the grin of disbelief on Captain Murphy's face, he decided to squeeze his way up the three short steps and onto the Harborview porch. It was true. There, in a tank in the window of the Harborview Fish House, was Big Claw himself, staring out at the crowd.

Mr. Languis, the owner of the fish house, was proudly tapping on the glass with his gold ring. "He's thirty-eight point seven pounds, and my guess is he's over forty years old."

Big Claw barely fit inside the tank. The hairy cilia on his legs looked like seaweed, and his shell was encrusted with barnacles. His crusher claw was forced up over his head. The claw itself must have weighed five pounds, its edges jagged like a knife. Inside the restaurant, little kids and even some adults were tapping at the tank, trying to get Big Claw's attention. A kid his age reached up and squeezed the tip of the crusher claw. Big Claw tried to pull away but couldn't. The kid laughed. His little sister laughed.

Maybe Big Claw remembered how he'd lost his other claw.

Maybe Big Claw thought he was going to be eaten.

Luther went inside.

"You're not going to eat him, are you, Mr. Languis?"

"That big lobster? Of course not. He draws the people in. I hope he'll last another forty years!" Mr. Languis carried an order to a table of diners, all of whom had lobster bibs tied underneath their chins. Luther leaned down to look at Big Claw. Big Claw just stared out the window toward the bay.

They held the clambake on the strip of beach in front of Uncle Bill's house. Being right on the beach was what made Uncle Bill's house so valuable. The house was always sort of a mess inside, but, as Uncle Bill put it, "I could raise pigs in there from October to May and still rent it out to the mainlanders." From the number of people that Luther saw packing the beaches on his bike ride over, he figured this was true. He'd nearly been hit by a moped and by a BMW with a Massachusetts license plate.

His mother had the jeep backed up to the flat rocks that lined the sandy part of the shore. In the back of the jeep were coolers full of quahogs, Uncle Bill's lobsters, fresh corn from the mainland, cherrystone clams, potatoes, lemons, big blocks of butter, and a brown bag full of parsley, onions, bay leaf, and sage. Luther looked out at the beach. Uncle Bill had dug the hole already. Beside it were two piles, one of driftwood and one of stone. They'd layer the pit with wood and stone, light it, then cook the food slowly in the fire.

Luther didn't see Jenny Swanson anywhere. He glanced quickly up at the house as he leaned his bike against his father's jeep. The sun and the ocean reflected in the windows. The bay was filled with sails. Luther's father had asked his mother to marry him during a sail, jumping into the water when she said yes. Luther liked to think of him this way, before he'd even known him, jumping into the water with his mother laughing and clapping her hands the way she did when she was happy.

"Luther!" Uncle Bill and his mother were hauling a big cooler down to the fire pit.

Luther hustled down to the beach.

The air had cooled. Some of the Swanson party was dancing now. The rest were roasting marshmallows in the embers of the fire pit. Luther was washing his hands in the ocean. He'd hauled a dozen trash bags full of shells and carcasses and gnawed corncobs up to the jeep, not to mention the recycling bags full of bottles and cans.

He'd watched Jenny Swanson for a lot of the clambake. Mostly she'd lain on a towel away from the rest of the party. Once he watched her swim. She'd come up from under a small wave coughing, like she'd swallowed water. She looked as if she didn't know where she was for a moment, and then she was looking straight at him. He wanted to talk with her, but he didn't have anything to say.

The water was warm around his hands, feet, and arms. He wanted to swim, but his mother had said he was to wait until he got home. He was an employee, not a guest, even if it was Uncle Bill's house. Near his toes, a bunch of hermit crabs were rolling around with the waves. One of them was too big for its shell. It would be looking for a new one soon. He picked it up. He felt the crab tickling his hand. He thought about Big Claw, all cooped up in his glass cage.

"You're the boy with the broken bicycle."

Luther turned. Jenny Swanson stood on the shore, not letting her feet get wet. She was holding a whole lobster tail that was split in two and dripping with butter.

The hermit crab dropped from Luther's hand. Luther

watched it float down through the water to the sand. "I had a flat." Luther didn't look up.

"My brother's got a BMX 9000. Maybe he'll let you ride it sometime."

Luther glanced at Jenny Swanson. She peeled some of the meat from the cracked lobster tail and put it in her mouth.

"I hate this island, don't you?" she said. "It's so boring." Butter dripped down her chin.

"I don't know," Luther said. And then he was walking quickly past her to his bike, resisting the urge to run. He knew what he had to do. His mother was sweeping the porch above the driveway. She called out Luther's name, but he did not answer. He got on his bike and sped away. He could phone Uncle Bill when he got home.

"He's a big lobster, isn't he?"

An elderly woman sat with her husband at the table in the Harborview Fish House nearest the tank. Luther tried to pretend he didn't hear her. Big Claw hadn't moved. Mr. Languis had put a filter and some sea plants in the tank, and a sign that read: "Big Claw—Monster from the Deep." Big Claw had positioned his head so that it was partially hidden by the plants.

Luther picked up the chair nearest him and set it next to the tank.

"Are you going to eat him up?" The woman was looking at Luther now. Luther was still in his shorts, and his t-shirt was stained with clam juice and wet with saltwater from the beach.

"No, ma'am," Luther said quickly. He had Kate's wagon just outside the door.

Luther wondered how much Jump Shot weighed; he'd picked her up before. He took a deep breath, sprang onto the chair, and plunged both arms down into the water. He tried not to think of what would happen if the plug slipped out of the crusher claw.

"Young man!" the old woman said, her eyes wide.

With one huge effort, Luther hoisted Big Claw from the tank, Big Claw's eight legs snapping, water splashing everywhere.

"Just a minute!" said her husband.

But Luther didn't stop. He charged out the restaurant door. He dropped Big Claw into the wagon. "Hold on, Big Claw," Luther said, and then he raced Kate's wagon across Ocean Avenue, rushing the lobster toward *Cathy's Cloud*.

Luther looked back once. Mr. Languis stood in the Fish House doorway, his arms folded across his chest.

Uncle Bill had the engine running. "Your mother's going to kill me," he hollered as he and Luther hurried the wagon onto the deck. Luther's heart was racing.

Cathy's Cloud sped away from the slip.

Luther watched Old Harbor get smaller, the people on the ferry dock and the crowded beaches shrinking, until he couldn't tell one person from another. Uncle Bill got on the CB radio and was laughing with someone as Luther wheeled the wagon toward the starboard edge. He carefully removed the wooden peg from the hinge of the crusher claw. And then he set Big Claw free.

꩜

Jeff W. Bens *was raised in Massachusetts and currently teaches in the film department at the University of North Carolina School of the Arts.*

Cape Cod Girls

This chantey was probably written sometime in the nineteenth century. It was designed to lift the spirits and boost the energies of men hauling up their ship's anchor as they prepared to take to the sea.

Cape Cod girls don't use no combs,
Haul away, haul away;
They comb their hair with a codfish bone,
And we're bound away for Australia.

REFRAIN:
So heave her up my bully, bully boys,
Haul away, haul away;
Heave her up and don't ya' make a noise,
And we're bound away for Australia.

Cape Cod kids don't have no sleds,
Haul away, haul away;
They slide down the hill on a codfish head,
And we're bound away for Australia.

[Refrain]

Cape Cod cats don't have no tails,
Haul away, haul away;
They lost 'em all in a Northeast gale,
And we're bound away for Australia.

[Refrain]

Cape Cod ladies don't have no frills,
Haul away, haul away;
They're plain and skinny as a codfish gill,
And we're bound away for Australia.

So heave her up my bully, bully boys,
Haul away, haul away;
Heave her up and don't ya' make a noise,
And we're bound away for Australia.

Of Beaches, Bays, and My Boyhood with the Colonel

William W. Warner

Although most visitors to the New Jersey shore favor its sandy beaches, budding adventurers can explore a wonderful variety of coastal habitats, including salt marshes, dunes, bays, tidal flats, and barrier beaches— thin strips of land that lie just off the coast.

Very little in my upbringing seems to have pointed toward a love for our great Atlantic beaches, much less writing about them. I was born and grew up in New York City in a house that was without great books, without a father, and for some periods of the year, without a mother. In *loco patris,* I had only a highly irascible step-grandfather. Colonel George Washington Kavanaugh was his name, and he wanted to be known by all of it. His most frequent utterance to me, apart from constant reminders that I was no blood kin, went something like this: "Your father is a bum, your mother is running around with every gigolo in Europe, so I suppose the spring can rise no higher than its source."

So much for the Colonel, as my brother and I always called him, and the genetic malediction he constantly laid on us. But there was one thing the Colonel did for us for which we are both eternally grateful. Come June every year he took our family, such as it was, to a place called Spring Lake, a summer resort on the New Jersey coast. Not that we especially liked the place. Our school mates all went "to the country" on vacations, and Spring Lake with its kiosked boardwalks, well-ordered streets, and great hotels with long porches and double rows of rocking chairs didn't seem very country to us. Reinforcing this impression was an institution known as the Bath and Tennis Club, where our contemporaries spent much of the day playing blackjack and sneaking cigarettes.

But at one end of the well-ordered streets, beyond the boardwalk and the great hotels, was an immense space. How immense I learned from my older brother, who at age nine or ten gave me my first taste for geography. "Look here," he said, showing me a world map and running his finger along the fortieth parallel, "there is nothing but the Atlantic Ocean between our beach and the coast of Portugal, four thousand miles away."

Suffice it to say that this bit of information, which was quite accurate, overwhelmed me. I soon began taking long walks along the beach, staring out at the ocean and dreaming of the day I might have a boat of my own to venture beyond the breakers and explore it. My brother shared this vision, although more in terms of a quest for better fishing. In due course we therefore built a crude box-shaped scow of heavy pine planking, painted it red, white, and green, and proudly named it the *Rex* after the great Italian ocean liner that was at the time one of the largest and most luxurious ships in the transatlantic passenger service. With the help of some of our huskier friends we grunted the *Rex* down the beach. The chosen day was fine, with a sprightly land breeze that did much to calm the breakers. Our plan was alternately to fish and paddle down to an inlet at the south end of Spring Lake that led into a small bay known as Wreck Pond. But after we were success-fully launched, our friends all laughing and cheering us on, we found the *Rex* to be something less than seaworthy and quite difficult to paddle. In fact, the sprightly western breeze that had made our passage through the surf so easy was now rapidly carrying us out to sea—straight for Portugal, I could not help thinking—with a strength against which our best efforts were no match. The reader can guess what followed. Alarms were sounded, authorities were sum-moned, and we were rescued. "One more trick like this and I'm cutting you out of my will," the Colonel said to us when we were brought home, humiliated, by the Coast Guard.

Nevertheless, before the sum-mer was over, my brother and I found we could ex-plore the incongruously named Wreck Pond well enough by foot and bicycle. It was, in fact, what biologists call a complete estuarine system, in miniature. At its mouth was the tide-scoured inlet, constantly shifting its sandy course. Behind the inlet was a shallow bay, a labyrinth of marsh islands, and ultimately, well inland, a freshwater stream fed by a millpond bordered by pin oak and magnolia. Thanks to this complex we could do everything from netting crabs and small fish to stalking the marsh flats looking for shore-birds, muskrat, or an occasional raccoon. We could even catch small trout up by the millpond dam, graciously provided by the New Jersey state fish hatcheries. What a relief these occasions offered from the Bath and Tennis Club, what an escape from the Colonel! Wreck Pond, in short, became our private world.

But there were other worlds to conquer, as the saying goes, in particular a large blank space on maps of the coast that my brother and I had both noticed and wondered about. It appeared as a long finger of land pointing southward, a mere ribbon of land between the Atlantic Ocean and Barnegat Bay. Most remarkably, the southern part of the finger, below a cluster of closely spaced beach resorts, showed no signs of human settlement nor even a road, as far as we could tell. (The reader will understand how rare this was when I say that even in the 1930s, which is the time I speak of, much of the New Jersey coast was already a solid corridor of resort townships.) The blank space was called Island Beach. It had to be investigated, we agreed.

For this greater enterprise we borrowed a canoe, provisioned it with three days' worth of canned pork and beans, and left an ambiguous note concerning our intentions on the Colonel's pillow. But once again the Aeolian gods did not favor us. This time a wet east wind slammed us against the marshes of Barnegat Bay's western shore, so strongly, in fact, that we found we could only gain ground by wading in the shallows and pushing and pulling the canoe. There was one bright moment in this otherwise dismal effort, however. After rounding a sharp bend in one of the marsh islands we came upon a sheltered and relatively quiet cove. There to our amazement were four or five mink cavorting down a mud slide they had excavated in the marsh bank. Over and over they shot down the slide—head first, tail first, on their stomachs, on their backs—to splash into the water with splendid abandon. Well hidden by the tall cordgrass, we watched transfixed as the mink evidently scrambled up an underwater burrow, reappeared above on the marsh bank, shook their silvery wet coats, and repeated the process. Forever, it seemed, or what must have been at least ten minutes. I have never forgotten the sight, nor seen another mink slide since.

We passed what seemed like a sleepless night huddled under a tump of bushes in the cordgrass that offered little cover from intermittent rains. The next morning we set out again, very tired, under a hazy sun and on glassy calm waters. Island Beach seemed almost in sight on the far horizon to the east, although it was hard to be sure in the haze. Just as we began to ponder the wisdom of continuing our journey, a large and official-looking motorboat with a slanted red stripe on its bow came alongside, bearing instructions to take us in tow. "That does it!" the Colonel said to us two hours later when we were brought home again, humiliated but grateful, by the Coast Guard. "I'm cutting you both out of my will."

A few years later, when I was sixteen and my brother and I had gone our separate ways, I got to Island Beach. I got there in what today is known as an ORV, or off-road vehicle. But mine was quite different from current models. Mine was a splendid little ORV, in fact, for which I make no apologies. Unknown to the Colonel I had acquired a lightweight Ford Model-T beach-buggy prototype with a chopped down body, painted in salt-resistant aluminum and equipped with four enlarged wheel rims and tires, all for the sum of fifty dollars. My buggy was totally incapable of sustained driving in soft sand, having only the standard two-wheel drive and a weak one at that. It therefore could never charge up dunes or otherwise alter the beach topography. To operate it successfully on Island Beach it was necessary to travel at low tide only, along the wet and more compact swash sand of the forebeach. This meant driving along close to the surf, constantly dodging the biggest waves, in what proved to be a thoroughly exhilarating experience. One could do this, moreover, for ten glorious miles, ten miles of wind-plumed breakers rolling in from the Atlantic, ten miles with seldom another human being in sight. Sometimes there would be schools of marauding bluefish just beyond the surf, marked by sprays of small fish breaking the surface and the screams of wheeling gulls and terns. In such event I would jam on the brakes (stepping on the reverse gear pedal worked even better), grab my cane surf rod, and heave out a heavy lead-squid lure as far as possible. If your cast went far enough, you got your blue. By the time you brought him in and unhooked him, you had to jump back into the buggy and race on to catch up with the fast-moving school. For a boy of sixteen these were moments of pure bliss, of feeling at one with the sea and the sand.

There were other attractions. Often I would leave my fishing companions to their patient pursuits and explore the back beach. The dunes of Island Beach were low, but with steep rampartlike faces on their seaward side. Behind the ramparts were small hollows of smooth sand marked only with the delicate circular tracings made by the tips of swaying dune grass. Then came beach heather and thickets of sea myrtle, stunted cedar, holly, and scrub oak. Gain the highest point of land, perhaps no more than twenty feet above sea level, and the small world of Island Beach lay revealed before you. On the one side were the choppy waves of Barnegat Bay at its broadest, bordered by salt marsh and tidal flats that attracted great numbers of both migrant and resident shorebirds. On the other were the dunes, the white sand, and the Atlantic breakers stretching away to a seeming infinity. It was a small world, easy to comprehend, and I loved it from the beginning.

William W. Warner *is the author of* Beautiful Swimmers: Watermen, Crabs, and the Chesapeake Bay, *which won a 1977 Pulitzer Prize,* Distant Water: The Fate of the North Atlantic Fisherman, *and* Into the Porcupine Cave and Other Odysseys: Adventures of an Occasional Naturalist. *He lives in Washington, D.C.*

Log of the *Downit*

ADRIAN KINGSBURY LANE

Adrian Kingsbury Lane grew up exploring the waters off Noank, Connecticut, in a small boat. His hobby was the start of something big: he grew up to become a ship captain and sail the major oceans of the world. The following are excerpts from the journal he kept between the ages of eleven and thirteen. We've kept his original spellings.

April 30, 1932

Went with father to Ram Island. The wind was southerly and blew hard. It was quite ruff. We sailed over in about 5 tacks and back in one. We brought back a cargo of muscles and we explored the island and went wading. We landed on the north end of the island and came home from there in eight mi[nutes].

May 14

Went to Mouse Island with Jack & Donn [the dog]. Used double power. Buried treasure and got a cargo of crockery. Then we visited West Ledge but found no gulls' eggs. We explored both places.

June 16, 1932

Cruised around in the river with the mate who went ashore and I went [on] to North Cove and picked up W.H.W. who went with me to Sixpenny Island which we explored. Then we explored a little on Goat Point and went under sail to the opposite shore. Then we went home, having a bad time putting through the bridge where the tide was against us. Wind was E.

June 18, 1932

The *Swan* towed us up the river to N Cove where we went for crabs but got none. Then we went further up the river and got a cargo of lumber at Sixpenny & Mason Islands where we explored.

P.M. The *Swan* towed us to Ram Island where we got a cargo of muscles.

June 21, 1932

I rowed alone to Ram Island to find my hunting knife which I lost on the voyage before. I went over in 20 minutes and found it. On the way back, spotted Fred Galley bound for the island for strawberries. I also got a cargo of fish from the *Alicia Estes*.

August 10, 1932

(Not sure of the date.) Went handlining with the mate for crabs by Bakers [Enders Is.] Cove Bridge near red buoy. We caught eight which we had cooked and ate for supper. We used four lines and caught lots of eggers. We rowed.

Sat. Aug. 5 P.M. [1933]

Louis, Father, Mother, Elizabeth D. [and I] went on a picnic up to Ram Pt. [Mason Is.] in the *Swan* and took my boat as a tender with the engine. When we were eating our dinner we heard the fire whistle and then saw some smoke at Rat Wilbur's dock. It was Loren Ellis's dragger *Idelie* which burned, injuring H. H. Park and others. The boat was not damaged very bad. Louis and I took my boat down to see the fire (after it was over). When we got down there the engine stopped and we had to row back. I couldn't start it because the gas wasn't on. There was no wind and we had to tow the *Swan* home with the engine on my boat. When Louis and I were going down to Noank [with the tow], we saw a sort of fin in the water which soon disappeared. We thought it might be a sand shark or something.

[No date.]

Norton Jamieson, Louis Bradford and I rowed up the river to see if we could see any sharks. We found a draw bucket adrift.

Aug. 30, 1933

Walter & I rowed to Mystic Island for the day. We took our dinner. We went swimming and sailed my schooner [working model] and explored the Is. There were quite a few people there. We were the second to arrive & the last to leave (except some campers who had borrowed our tent). Walter tried to catch fish on a safety pin. We didn't succeed, but we got some muscles. We got some golden rod.

Sat. Sept. 30, 1933

The *Swan* and my boat went to F.I. [Fishers Island] where my boat was used to go ashore. We had the engine and towed the *Swan* part way over and most of the way back. The rest of the time the *Swan* towed my boat. We went down the Is. and up on top of Chocomont from where with my spyglass we could see the houses on Block Island and the lighthouse on Montauk Pt. We saw a two-masted lumber schooner going down the Sound when we were coming over. It was moon light when we got home. We saw some porpoise coming over.

Saturday. July 14 [1934]

Norton and I rowed over to Mason Is. We went up the creek and into the woods but found only green huckleberries. Then we went as much farther as we could and went up on the hill where we picked a quart of high bush blueberries and did some exploring. We had never been there before.

❧

Adrian Kingsbury Lane *was a lieutenant in the U.S. Coast Guard during World War II, then spent sixteen more years skippering sailing vessels, including the world's largest sailing ketch, the* R/V Atlantis, *which he sailed for the Woods Hole Oceanographic Institute.*

A Summer in Brewster

HELEN KELLER

Helen Keller was born in Alabama in 1880. When she was seventeen months old, she fell ill with a fever that left her blind and deaf. She was later taught to communicate through sign language and to read braille. The following excerpt, taken from an autobiography written when Helen Keller was a sophomore in college, recounts an episode that occurred when she was eight years old.

Just before the Perkins Institution closed for the summer, it was arranged that my teacher and I should spend our vacation at Brewster, on Cape Cod, with our dear friend, Mrs. Hopkins. I was delighted, for my mind was full of the prospective joys and of the wonderful stories I had heard about the sea.

My most vivid recollection of that summer is the ocean. I had always lived far inland and had never had so much as a whiff of salt air; but I had read in a big book called "Our World" a description of the ocean which filled me with wonder and an intense longing to touch the mighty sea and feel it roar. So my little heart leaped high with eager excitement when I knew that my wish was at last to be realized.

No sooner had I been helped into my bathing-suit than I sprang out upon the warm sand and without thought of fear plunged into the cool water. I felt the great billows rock and sink. The buoyant motion of the water filled me with an exquisite, quivering joy. Suddenly my ecstasy gave place to terror; for my foot struck against a rock and the next instant there was a rush of water over my head. I thrust out my hands to grasp some support, I clutched at the water and at the seaweed which the waves tossed in my face. But all my frantic efforts were in vain. The waves seemed to be playing a game with me, and tossed me from one to another in their wild frolic. It was fearful! The good, firm earth had slipped from my feet, and everything seemed shut out from this strange, all-enveloping element—life, air, warmth and love. At last, however, the sea, as if weary of its new toy, threw me back on the shore, and in another instant I was clasped in my teacher's arms. Oh, the comfort of the long, tender embrace! As soon as I had recovered from my panic sufficiently to say anything, I demanded: "Who put salt in the water?"

After I had recovered from my first experience in the water, I thought it great fun to sit on a big rock in my bathing-suit and feel wave after wave dash against the rock, sending up a shower of spray which quite covered me. I felt the pebbles rattling as the waves threw their ponderous weight against the shore; the whole beach seemed racked by their terrific onset, and the air throbbed with their pulsations. The breakers would swoop back to gather themselves for a mightier leap, and I clung to the rock, tense, fascinated, as I felt the dash and roar of the rushing sea!

Helen Keller *devoted her life to social reform for people with disabilities, writing twelve books and winning numerous national and international honors.*

Great Places

Where the River Meets the Sea

JOHN FRANK

The winding current reaches wide
where the river meets the sea.
The air draws scent from the salted tide
where the river meets the sea.
The marsh grass sways from side to side,
the mud flats foam where the mollusks hide,
the herons fly in a long low glide
where the river meets the sea.

John Frank *resides in Kirkland, Washington, and is the author of*
three books for children.

The Magic of the Flats

CLARE LEIGHTON

Mud flats are the vast plains you see along certain shorelines at low tide. Flat and a bit drab, they're not the sort of places most people find immediately attractive. But in this essay, Clare Leighton describes the wonders of the mud flats in such a way as to make just about anyone want to stop and take a closer look.

The best time to learn the world of the flats comes at the full of the moon. Then, for a few days in the Bay of Cape Cod, the big tides run high—nearly twelve feet at their peak—and, with the correspondingly extreme low, the water retreats far into the bay, exposing land that is never seen over the rest of the month.

This dramatically low tide occurs early in the day, when the morning light is clean and clear, giving a pearly beauty to the world.

The mud flats are forsaken and desolate, frequented only by a scattering of quahog rakers. During the summer, when the Cape is filled with vacationists, you seldom find any of the visitors out there. To them the sea is something in which to swim. When it withdraws from them at low tide, they wait until the water returns. And this is fortunate, for some of the special quality of the flats lies in the eerie solitude.

The flats hold a subtle, rather than an obvious, beauty. It is the beauty of uncountable gradations of tone and hue, of the sheen and polish of exposed wet sand at low water. It is a world of reflections upon the wet sand from the slanted light of the morning sky.

There is a sense of vastness on such a morning. This stretch of mud and sand, merging imperceptibly in the far distance into remote water, seems to extend into eternity. In such a light, time and space become intermingled; we can no longer distinguish one from the other.

But it is not only the muted, opalescent coloring of the wet sand, shimmering and glinting upon the bed of the withdrawn ocean, that holds such magic. There are uncountable variations of form here, too. For this is the whole earth in microcosm, with Lilliputian valleys and hills, gorges and plateaux. . . .

And then we walk out on these flats, so muddy that the feet sink deep beneath the surface, into soft black ooze. Seen from a distance they appear devoid of all life, and all interest. But what do we discover? This is no dead world of mud. It is a living, agitated world, filled with pulsating rhythm and movement. Scarcely anything here lies motionless, except the long-vacated, sharp-edged shells of oysters and clams, clumped upright in the wet sand and looking as prehistoric as Stonehenge.

Stand still in your path across this mud. The flats appear to move. They heave. They vibrate. And then you hear a strange sound against the silence around. . . .

Puzzled, I raise my eyes to the flats. Thin jets of water spout before me, like tiny fountains. The air sparkles as the sun catches them, tossing into them the colors of the rainbow. Sometimes they are flung far, and this spectrum-tinted water, bewitched by the early morning sun, describes great arcs across the mud.

What is it that causes this crazy happening?

It is the scallops. They lie here, countless in their numbers.

At this moment, when I am confused, still, by sight and sound and strange recollections from the past, the shellfish warden approaches me across the flats.

"A good scallop year," he informs me blandly, not knowing how he has smashed my fantasies. "Never seen so many scallops—not for years I haven't. Looks to me as if we'll have a real bumper season, come October and they've grown."

And then I see what is happening. It is a world of *Alice in Wonderland*, with the Walrus and the Carpenter and the Oysters. The uncountable scallops assume a fairy-tale quality, till you would feel little surprise were they suddenly to develop legs and feet and should walk and talk. They open and shut their shells, like a multitude of castanets, like a gigantic audience applauding the beauty of this earth on such a morning in late June.

But, too, they have a rude aspect to their behavior; they spit, as they open, in the manner of vulgar old men. They yawn, exposing that mighty muscle which is the part that we eat. Along the rim of each beautiful fluted shell they boast a row of brilliant turquoise-blue, green-edged, jewel-like eyes. Give them the slightest kick as they lie here in the mud at low tide, and they will retaliate by spitting you in the face. They imagine they are beneath the water, still, opening and shutting to breathe and propel themselves along the bay.

The scallop is never static. It is far more active and flexible than the heavy, uncouth quahog that noses its way downward into the mud and sand of the water bed. It has an adventurous spirit. The entire bay is its universe. And it is as beautiful of shape as it is mobile of movement, a delicate, graceful creature, the fluted shells subtly varied in color. And with this beauty it carries, too, the sense of history in its background; for did not the pilgrims of the Middle Ages adopt it as their symbol of pilgrimage?

Sometimes this sucking sound changes to a wheezing, squeezing noise, as the scallops force out the water before them, the better to propel themselves along. They do not even await disturbance, as does the razor fish, but act independently of all outside happenings.

Nothing is still here upon the flats, except the discarded clam and oyster shells; and even these ancient creatures are peopled with tiny sea snails perching on top of them, like Kings of the Castle in the game of a child. Over the floor of the sea swarm the hermit crabs, so minute and so active, trotting around on nervous little feet, or retiring into their shells to get sucked down deep into the bed of the wet sand. They creep among the colorless slabs of jellyfish, and the stranded shells, dull of hue against the rich scarlet of the frilly edged sponge that encrusts the oysters and clams.

. . . I walk further out into the bay, to join a friend who is raking for quahogs.

We scratch the surface of the mud

at the water's edge, or even down into the water-covered channels, for the hard-shelled clam, the quahog, as it is called on the Cape from the days when the Indians lived here and prized it as their food. It is an exciting harvest, like all harvests of the unseen. It is charged with speculation, like the digging of potatoes. Something hard resists the rake and you haul it up, secure between the prongs: there is your quahog. Or you dip your hand down into the muddied water—this water that blackens as you disturb it with the rake or with your feet—and bring it up. The wire basket, sitting there on the bed of the channel, three quarters submerged below the water, grows heavy with the quahogs. We lift it and place it near to our center of operation, as we move across the flats.

When the basket is full to the brim, we carry it to our staked bed. Scratching a shallow hole in the mud, we stick the quahogs vertically down, scarcely below the surface. The bed has the appearance of a vegetable garden, out here at sea, with its orderly rows. They might almost be onions that we plant, or daffodil bulbs. And now, as we place the clams into their new home, we watch them. After the first moment of stunned resistance they start to react according to their nature. With a gentle rocking movement they get themselves sucked down below the surface of the mud, drawing in their siphons and shutting their shells as they force out the water inside them in tiny jets. Come back here in a few more minutes and you will see nothing. They will have vanished below, settling themselves flat within their muddy beds. And all that can be seen will be the oyster shells, planted in this bed, shabby-colored and ancient-looking, so hoary of texture that they seem to antedate time.

The world of the flats has a seasonal element, every bit as

much as though it were the vegetable world of dry land, with the blooming and ripening of fruit or grain. The "set" of the oyster takes place in the spring or the early summer, and the little scallops in the bay reach maturity only in October. June and July pass, and I wander over the flats at the end of August. The morning is foggy. I seem to move in space, like a figure in an early Chinese landscape. I have lost all sense of dimension or element. It is already daylight, but the fog makes me recollect a walk I took many years before, at dusk, when the fog rolled in with the suddenness of the dropping of the curtain at the end of a play. That evening, as I stood there upon the flats, well out into the bay, I felt myself to be living upon an uninhabited planet. It was as I would imagine it to be, were I to wander upon the surface of the moon. My feet sank deep into mud, plunging to the calves of my legs. My mind knew that this was black mud, though my eyes could see little of the color. I waded into channels of water, to the knees, water filled with unperceived crabs. And suddenly, as I stood there, knee-deep in water and mud, I felt panic. It was an unashamed, animal panic, the terror of complete loss of direction, an aloneness in space, with the tide turning and the sea advancing, and my not knowing exactly where to walk. In this eerie, scarifying world, formless and lightless, extending into fog, blurred by fog and darkening dusk, I stood still. I searched the sky, but above me was nothing but fog.

"Stupid," I found myself saying. "Nobody in their senses would have done such an idiotic thing. Why, perhaps I'll have to stay here till the incoming tide, with the water lapping higher and higher up my legs and thighs. That will show me where I am. Then I can walk away from it. . . . But suppose I go in circles, as people are supposed to do when they are lost?"

In a queer way I found something exciting in the sense of utter loneliness. I knew that if I were to manage to reach land, I would have experienced something that was worth this panic and fear.

But things always seem to turn out right in the end. At the moment when panic was beginning to envelop me, I stood completely still and very slowly turned myself around. There must have been a sudden break in the thickening fog, for I saw a light in the distance before me. I walked towards it, my eyes fixed upon it, regardless of whether I trod upon crab or sharp-edged oyster shell, or sank deep to my knees in mud. I shall never know how long it took me to reach shore, for I had forsaken the habitual world of dry land, with its sense of time. But I fastened my eyes to that solitary light, till finally I found my feet were treading safely on sand.

All this has come back to me, as I wander across the flats on a foggy morning in late August. But it is a thin fog today, simplifying the curves of Egg Island, dark gray against the silver water. At any moment it will lift, disclosing the form of the flats and the patterning of the cool, swift-running channels. I cross Egg Island, to the far edge, past the green-tinged part that is covered with tattered sea lettuce, and the desolate, lifeless mud gives way to the strangest accumulation of razor fish shells. My feet crunch upon them, in their thousands, mud-obscured, lying there at all angles. And I wonder why it should be that they are here at this particular spot, and nowhere else. . . .

It is rich, varied, and beautiful, this world of the flats, this low-tide country of sand and mud. It may lack the dramatic violence of the Atlantic, but if you look closely at it, and stand still and listen, it will disclose immeasurable magic.

Clare Leighton *was born in London in 1898 and moved to the United States when she was forty. She spent many summers in Wellfleet, Massachusetts. A talented woodcut engraver, she illustrated her own books and many classics, and designed the stained-glass windows for the Wellfleet Methodist Church.*

Cranberry Cove

MÉLINA BROWN

Although wild cranberries were probably served at the first Thanksgiving, the cranberry we now eat—the American, or large, cranberry—is culti- vated. Cranberry cultivation began in Massachusetts in the early nine- teenth century and later spread to New Jersey, where this story takes place. When the cranberries are ready for harvesting, the fields are flooded, and brilliant red berries rise to the surface.

"Hop in the car," Dad said with a huge smile. He extended his arm in front of the door of a new, royal blue BMW, like those glittery women do on game shows.

"Where did you get the car, Dad?" I asked, noticing the shine of the body as well as the hubcaps. We usually rode the bus.

"Never mind. . . . It's ours for the weekend. Put your bag in- side and let's go for a ride!"

We cruised out of Atlantic City, leaving the high-rise ho- tels, casino billboards, neon lights, and car exhaust fumes be- hind. Living so close to the ocean would be great, if I could actually be next to it more. But Mama is always working at the restaurant and worries about me going places without her.

Sometimes I meet Dad near the casino where he works, and we walk along Atlantic City's famous boardwalk. It's not a bad place in the fall and winter. Even though seagulls are always screaming for food, you can smell a salty freshness in the air and feel a misty wind on your face. Frothy waves crash against the sand. But in the summer, zillions of tourists polka dot the beach and the air smells like popcorn, tanning oil, old cologne, dead fish, fried fish, french fries, and damp sand.

I was excited now about going out of town with Dad, but awfully curious. Even though it was my weekend to spend with him, we usually didn't go away. I wondered if Mama would be happy to have a long weekend to herself or if she'd be nervous about me going out of town without her.

"Where are we going?" I asked as we crossed another bridge.

"You'll see soon enough," was all Dad said before his curly black mustache stretched into another wide smile.

We watched the scene change from tall, shiny hotels to cottagelike motels to farmhouses and fields. But neither of us said a word. We just listened to the hip-hop beat blasting through custom speakers. This was some ride!

Trees appeared alongside the road, taller than the ones in town. We were on Route 563, headed toward the Pinelands. At least that's what the sign said. The sky opened up a bit and I noticed wavy hills, like sand dunes, only with less sand. A couple of hours later, Dad pulled onto a small, sandy road and we headed farther north. Then he stopped the car and said, "Let's stretch a bit."

I grabbed my jacket, even though it was pretty warm for October. I followed Dad's every move, not sure where we were going or why.

We walked through a mushy field of tall grass, almost up to my waist. I'm tall for a sixth grader, but nowhere near as tall as

Dad. This grass was high! Dad clamped my shoulder lightly, like he does when he's got something serious to tell me—like when he and Mama got divorced. "Troy," he had said then, "your mama and me are breaking up." As though they were only going together or something.

I wondered if he'd say something that serious this time too. But he didn't say anything. We walked on. I saw him looking at some tall trees with peeling strips of white and gray bark, like wisps of hair.

"That's paper birch," he said without looking at me.

His hand left my shoulder and he turned to watch a tall, skinny bird take off from its hiding place in a tuft of grass. When the bird fluttered and flapped its steel gray wings, it looked gawky. Its spindly legs stuck out behind it. But seconds later it was in the air, its long needlelike beak guiding it in a graceful glide. Dad noticed me noticing the bird.

"That's a blue heron," he explained.

I wondered how he knew the names of these things. He'd worked in the casino as long as I could remember.

The ground grew squishier and small pools of tea-colored water appeared. It was swampy, but not full of crocodiles or creepy creatures like swamps in the movies. It was open and wide here, not spooky at all.

"We're close now," Dad said.

"Close to what?" My heart was beating fast. I couldn't figure out where we were going.

"You'll see," was all Dad offered.

He's still smiling, I thought. So it can't be all that bad, whatever it is.

The air smelled fresh and piney, and just a little salty—different from the fishy food and exhaust smell of Atlantic

City. We climbed a small, sandy dune. Once at the top, I stopped and caught my breath. Dad turned to see my reaction as I looked down below.

A small sea of red stretched before me. Tiny, bright, red beads bobbed on top of the water. Sun sparkled through open patches, and it was so pretty it made me smile. I'd never seen such a spread of red.

"What is that, Dad?"

He laughed at me as though I'd made a joke. "Cranberries, Troy, my boy!" He laughed again. "That's where your cranberry jelly comes from."

I thought back to Thanksgiving, the last time I'd had cranberries. I'd been with Mama and her folks, Aunt Treecie and Uncle Clarence, and Serina. We'd had only the canned cranberry jelly, not the fresh cranberries Dad had always insisted on when he had lived with us. I never knew where they'd come from though.

We walked down closer to the water and I could see the details I'd missed. Small clusters of candy red berries floated and waved as the wind rippled through the water. They reminded me of tiny Christmas tree ornaments and lights decorating the swamp. I wondered if I'd become cranberry colored if I jumped in.

"Bet you never knew your dad used to come here all the time," Dad said, smiling again and turning to me for my reaction.

I didn't know what to say. So I waited for his explanation.

"You know I was born in Newark. But I grew up over here, in Burlington County."

I was surprised that he'd grown up here and I'd never known it. But was that why he brought me here?

"I used to love coming here when I was a boy," he went on. "Spring would come, and I'd pick me some blossoms from the bog when no one was looking. They looked like pink ribbons all curled up. We weren't supposed to mess with them, because that's what brings the money in—these cranberries. But, you gotta have a little fun. Know what I'm saying?"

He waited for me to answer, and I nodded my head. I wondered if he'd just brought me here to see where he used to live, or if there was more he had to tell me.

"Your grandfather, my father—it's too bad you didn't get to meet him before he died—he used to be a picker. Hard work, standing in the cold water all day. They use these big, blue roller-beater-like machines now, to get the berries off the stems and floating onto the water. They look kind of like over-sized lawn mowers."

Dad crouched down near the water and picked up a berry. He shook it in his fist and turned toward me again.

"Troy," he started, and I knew it was coming—the news he'd brought me here for. "I've decided to leave the city. Get away from that gambling life. Find me another job."

He eyed me with concern as my eyes widened with surprise. "I met someone, Troy. She's from here, too, and wants me to move back."

I let out a breath, relieved that he didn't have an incurable illness, or another son, or anything else. But this also meant he'd never get back together with Mama.

"Hey, little man. Don't look so shocked. It's not that far! You saw how long it took us to get here—barely a couple of hours." He tapped me under my chin. Usually, he does that to make me look down, and when I do, he laughs, "Gotcha! Made you look!" This time he didn't.

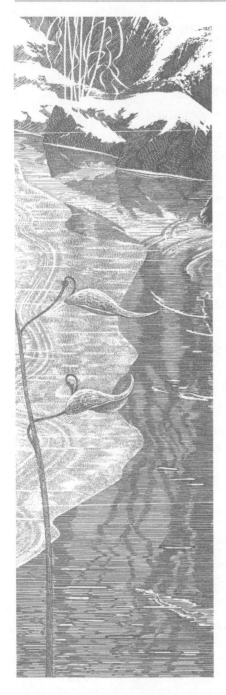

"Will I still get to see you?" I asked him.

"Course you will, Troy. That's not going to change. We'll still see each other just as much as we do now, and maybe even more, depending on what kind of job I find. And," he added with a smile, "you'll get to come here." He spread his arms wide, as if he were the King of Cranberries, and this was his kingdom.

He looked happier than I re-membered seeing him in a long time, and I felt a little better, knowing I wouldn't lose him. I picked up a couple of berries and shook them in my fist as he'd done. Then I smiled.

"Soooo, what's her name?"

"*Now* you're interested in my life, hmmm? Well, I'm glad. She's a very nice woman." Dad smiled again.

"Aren't you going to tell me her name?" I asked, shaking the fist full of cranberries faster.

"She works at the state park, and—hey, don't cream me with cranberries!" Dad laughed and ran as I showered him with the remaining cranberries in my hand. He chased me as I scrambled up the hill, then lightly tackled me from behind. But instead of throwing me to the ground, he turned me around in a hug.

"Everything will work out, Troy. You'll see. Cranberries aren't that bad, are they?"

I nodded and smiled back, wondering what else I might discover about Dad, or about this land outside the city I never knew existed.

Mélina Brown *was born in France, raised in Minnesota, and reincarnated in North Carolina. She attended the College of St. Thomas, the Sorbonne, and the University of North Carolina at Chapel Hill. Ms. Brown works as a school librarian much of the year and has written pieces that have appeared in* Library Talk, Life Notes: Personal Writings by Contemporary Black Women, *and* Women's Words: A Journal of Carolina Writing.

Seascape

April Lindner

At low tide you can wade the cove
from Revere to Nahant, the warmed Atlantic
licking your knees, clouds of red algae
clinging to your calves. Along the damp
and wrinkled sand, sea worms curl
into pale rosettes, so many
they're difficult to miss. Keep leaning
against the current, trying to forget
the boulders worried down to rocks,
to pebbles, to the silt that wants
to suck you under. Let your feet
brush bottle tops and gutted clams
diminishing in the alchemy
of salt. A few miles out
a garbage scow shuttles its load,
dusky and slow as a seafaring mountain
against the bright sky. Keep north,
pocking the mud with temporary footprints
past gray-capped birds, half-breeds
of pigeon and gull, each one
declaring a small kingdom
with a stretch of its pterodactyl wings.

April Lindner, *who once lived on the north shore of Massachusetts, now teaches English at Wittenberg University in Ohio.*

Three Trees in the City

CECILE MAZZUCCO-THAN

Many of us visit beaches or protected areas to experience the natural wonders of the North Atlantic Coast. But what kinds of life can we find right outside our doors? In this essay, Cecile Mazzucco-Than shares her memories of city trees and a backyard wilderness.

I grew up in Bridgeport, Connecticut, a city of 130,000 people and three sixty-foot oak trees whose trunks were each about four feet in diameter. Actually, my neighborhood was lucky enough to have lots of trees, many of them oaks, but none were as big and beautiful as the three that stood in front of my parents' house.

The canopies of our three trees combined to form a dense shade that kept our house and front yard cool all summer. At twilight, my aunt would walk over from her own house two doors away, to sit on the shaded stoop with my parents and talk. My cousins and I hid behind the trees and ran around them. Although the front lawn was mostly mushrooms and moss, it was our stage and the trees were our biggest props. They were also our biggest fans. On summer evenings while our parents chatted quietly, we presented our three-person interpretation of *The Wizard of Oz*, and the trees applauded with a cool breeze.

In the autumn we'd rake up a haystack-high pile of leaves to jump in. Then we'd gather acorns and my dad would help us hollow them out—big ones for Popeye pipes and little ones that could fit in the caps of larger acorns for sets of Barbie dishes. If I was playing on the corner with my cousins when the sun went down and the streetlights flickered on, I ran toward the silhouette of a small house nestled under three giant trees.

When I was in fourth grade, my cousins and I used to sit on webbed lawn chairs in the garage during the summer thunderstorms and watch through the open door as the trees groaned and swayed in the wind. My cousins recounted certain scientific studies they had read proving oak trees attracted lightning. I always shivered appreciatively, but I knew these "scientific studies" were no more believable than a good ghost story.

When I began to read poetry, the trees became the village blacksmith's spreading chestnut or Evangeline's murmuring pines and hemlocks. Seeing the trees in the summer sunshine I could imagine the majesty of Ashley Wilkes's Twelve Oaks, and on a foggy Halloween night I could feel the terror of Ichabod Crane's lonely ride through Sleepy Hollow.

My dad had seen those same three oak trees when he was growing up in Bridgeport during the mid-1920s, long before our home was built, when the trees were part of a forest surrounding a small lake that my dad and his friends used to swim in. A stream and a waterfall connected it to a much larger lake only a few miles away. In those days, the larger lake served as a reservoir supplying drinking water to a large part of the city, and the small lake helped maintain the water level in the reservoir and prevent flooding in times of heavy rain.

The area around both lakes was protected, and my dad and his friends always ran the risk of being chased away. My dad had seen a different city, one where forests, lakes, and farmlands began at the end of the bus line. Where I saw rows of post-war Cape Cod homes, my dad had seen forests of American chestnut, walnut, and hazelnut.

I guess we were lucky the developer who built our house resolved to work around the three oaks. I don't know if developers were more conscientious in 1942, but they decided to preserve the small lake also. Despite the nearness of Main Street and the houses that crowded around the lake and side streets, I knew the joy of jumping into the clear water on a hot summer's day. The three trees and the lake brought *Wild Kingdom* out of my television set and into my backyard. Little fishes nipped my legs as I floated in the water. I watched painted turtles sun themselves on the concrete steps of the neighbor's landing, and I listened to bull frogs and crickets sing in the evening. Mallard ducks ate the bread I tossed to them and built their nests in the brambles around the roots of the huge, twisted old willow trees at the water's edge. I watched as the ducks defended their eggs from the muskrats, who were invisible except for the v-shaped ripples that they made as they swam through the water. Squirrels built nests in the oak trees, crows cackled from their topmost branches, and a red-winged blackbird swooped down on anyone that dared walk under the high branch in one of the gnarled willows that cradled his nest.

When I was about eight or nine years old, my dad and I salvaged a half-submerged, ten-foot aluminum rowboat that had been floating in the lake for several weeks. We pulled it out of the water, across our landing, and into the backyard. We patched the hole in its bottom with metal plates, rubber gaskets, and short, sturdy carriage bolts. My father found oarlocks and a pair of oars and taught me to row. Soon my cousins and I could follow the turtles and the muskrats along the rocky banks of the lake.

We loved to glide across the lake to the opposite bank where three huge weeping willows grew so close to the water's edge that tough, red, stringy webs of their roots pushed through the stones lining the lake's banks and floated in thick, wide clumps on top of the water. We called it the Sargasso Sea. The roots made it almost impossible to dip the oars into the water, and the boat nearly beached itself on them as if they were sandbars. The willows' heavy branches sent hundreds of very thin, bright yellow, flexible branches cascading towards the water's surface. Each of these ribbonlike branches sported thousands of pairs of long, thin, lozenge-shaped leaves, pale green on one side and silver on the other, attached so tenuously to each branch that they danced in the wind. We loved to row under these branches and let them trail across the boat as we slowly moved through them. We pretended we were deep in the bayou with its trees dripping with Spanish moss.

I never realized how unique my experience of growing up in the city had been until many years later when I brought a friend from college home with me for a short visit. She grew up in Barcelona, one of the largest and most beautiful cities in all of Spain. When I told her I lived in the largest city in Connecticut, she thought she would feel at home. Barcelona, she said, is a city of cars and scooters, apartment buildings, shops, and churches. So is Bridgeport, I replied. As we rode the Main Street bus from the railroad station in the center of the downtown business district up to the North End where I lived, she could see from the shops, tall buildings, and apartment complexes that the cities were similar. However, once we got off the bus and walked up and down the side streets to the street where I lived, she thought my home was in the middle of a city park.

I introduced her to all my childhood joys. We sat on the front porch in the shade of the three oak trees; we rowed the boat into the Sargasso Sea and shivered as the curtains of Spanish moss trailed over us. I showed her how to hold a piece of bread in her hands and let the mallard ducks snatch it from her fingertips. Each time, she pulled her fingers back and squealed. Although Barcelona has many parks, she'd never done anything like this in the city.

She'd never seen trees as tall and strong as the three oaks that stood in front of our house, either. I told her how a fourth-grade Sunday school class inspired me to name them Shadrach, Mesach, and Abednego. The three trees refused to yield to the yards and asphalt streets and concrete sidewalks that surrounded them, threatened to knock them down and cover them over in the name of clean and progressive city life. Their tenacity reminded me of the Old Testament story of Daniel's three friends who stood firm in their faith and survived being thrown into an inferno. For the next twenty years as I grew up and went to high school, then college, and finally graduate school, I remained their Daniel fighting to save them from neighbors who would rather cut them down and burn their limbs than rake the leaves that fell from their branches in autumn.

While I lived with my parents and afterward when I returned home from college and grad school for summer vacations and holidays, I was forest ranger, conservationist, and arborist—the only obstacle between them and the fiery furnace—tirelessly raking their fallen leaves in October and urging our neighbors to enjoy the cool breeze and dense shade under their canopy in July. And then, when I was twenty-nine years old, I married a man with a job in another state. I knew I'd have to move away from my parents' home forever. Since my dad had passed away some years before and my mom couldn't live alone, I knew she'd have to move with us. That meant we'd have to sell my parents' home and with it, the three trees. And I wasn't sure the new owners would understand the importance of preserving them.

If Nationwide moved trees, I would have taken them with me. Before we packed up my mother's furniture and sold my parents' home, I even tried to think of a way to get the trees on a historical preservation list. I hoped the U.S. Department of the Interior would take over where I left off and the National Park Service would send over a forest ranger from time to time to check on them. Even at nearly thirty years old, I guess I was a bit naive about how unimportant very small and privately owned green space must seem to a federal government already overburdened by more pressing issues such as crime, poverty, and unemployment, and perhaps spoiled by the vast public riches of national parks such as Yosemite or the Grand Canyon.

However, my idea of getting the trees on a historical preservation list wasn't without precedent. I remembered a long-ago third grade field trip when the class piled into a sawed-off school bus and rode to the naked side of the city to look at a one hundred-year-old tree. It didn't have any notable history—not like the Charter Oak in Hartford. This tree was just a tree that had managed to survive despite the factories and six-family houses, the concrete and asphalt, and the dented Chevys double-parked between sidewalk and curb. It was big and gnarled, and its roots had twisted up beneath the pavement, lifting the concrete in places. We looked at it in wonder, and I remember being sure that my three oaks, though taller and straighter, were at least as old. But this tree was somehow put on a historical preservation list, and mine were not.

Although I have never returned to my former home, I heard from some well-meaning relatives that the people who bought our house cut down the three oak trees. The reason the new owners gave was that they owned several vehicles, but only one could fit in our garage. I'm sure at first they tried to wedge their pickup between one tree and the stockade fence the neighbor put up twenty years ago to keep our leaves from blowing onto her lawn. Then, after a backbreaking autumn of raking leaves, they might have rationalized that the trees took up space that could be used to park their truck, extra passenger car, and oversized camper. Without out the trees, they could drive their vehicles right up to the side door and park them in a neat row.

I cannot imagine my parents' home without

the three oak trees or how anyone could look at their stumps and feel anything but pain. When I remember the trees now, seven years after I moved away from them, I remember my wedding day, the day the trees greeted me for the last time. I wore my mother's wedding gown of post-war satin the color of candlelight. As I stepped out the front door and onto the porch where my parents and my aunt had sat and watched us play so many years ago, the trees applauded once again, rustling in the cool breeze. Our neighbor across the street dropped his rake and ran inside his house to get his camera. I waited on the porch. On what truly was the happiest day of my life, in my mind I had to say good-bye to my three old friends.

When my husband brought his relatives back to my parents' house after the wedding, they couldn't stop looking at the three oak trees. One uncle walked halfway down the street to take a picture of one tree from root to crown. Some of these relatives came from Europe, long ago deforested. Others came from Malaysia, where a supercity squeezes the jungle, and others from Aruba, where no tree is taller than the squat divi-divi permanently bowed to the island breeze. None of them would have sacrificed one of our oaks for an additional parking spot.

While the wonders of the natural world from Malaysia to Aruba are showcased on *National Geographic*, the trees cut down in the city go unnoticed. In the shade of the oak trees and the cool of the pond, I learned to breathe deeply and tread softly and look at the natural world with awe and reverence while living in the largest city in Connecticut. This was my Amazon and my Sahara, a place as fragile and ecologically important as the rain forest or the desert. Perhaps, if Shadrach, Mesach, and Abednego had appeared on television, if the Discovery channel had told their story, they might have lived on to provide the new owner's children with Popeye pipes and Barbie dishes, piles of autumn leaves to jump into, and applause for the dreams playacted in their shade.

Cecile Mazzucco-Than, *her husband, and her mom now live in Massachusetts in a home surrounded by a dozen sixty-foot pine trees. She has been writing since she was ten years old, and her essays have been published in popular magazines as well as scholarly journals.*

In New Jersey Once

MARIA MAZZIOTTI GILLAN

In New Jersey once, marigolds grew wild.
Fields swayed with daisies.
Oaks stood tall on mountains.
Powdered butterflies graced the velvet air.

Listen. It was like that.
Before the bulldozers.
Before the cranes.
Before the cement sealed the earth.

Even the stars, which used to hang
in thick clusters in the black sky,
even the stars are dim.

Burrow under the blacktop,
under the cement; the old dark earth
is still there. Dig your hands into it,
feel it, deep, alive on your fingers.

Know that the earth breathes and pulses still.
Listen. It mourns. In New Jersey once, flowers grew.

Maria Mazziotti Gillan *is the founder and director of the Poetry Center at Passaic County Community College in Paterson, New Jersey, editor of the* Paterson Literary Review, *and coeditor with her daughter Jennifer Gillan of* Unsettling America: An Anthology of Contemporary Multicultural Poetry *(Viking/Penguin),* Identity Lessons: Contemporary Writing about Learning to be American *(Penguin/Putnam), and* Growing Up Ethnic in America *(Penguin/Putnam). This poem describes her memories of the neighborhood in Paterson where she lived as a child.*

New Hampshire Shore: Haiku

DIANE MAYR

low tide line—
footprints fill with water
washing me away

on the rocks
humming tunes for
periwinkles

roots grasp cliff
as if to balance leaves
pointing seaward

sandcastles
and mayflies gone
in a day

sea glass—
human debris returns
as treasure

found:
mermaid's purse empty
of its riches

Diane Mayr *has spent the past twenty-five years in New Hampshire and loves its eighteen miles of Atlantic coast. She's been a children's librarian for more than a dozen years and a writer for nearly as long. The mother of two children, Ms. Mayr also shares the house with two cats.*

The Fog Maiden's Necklace

GERALDINE MARSHALL GUTFREUND

Geologists say the islands of Maine are the tops of mountains and hills that have been submerged by the rising sea. But we like this explanation just as much.

Around the land of Maine are islands large and small, scattered in the sea as though they had been strewn haphazardly from the sky. Some days there is a misty gray fog that enfolds the land like a veil, and it is on these days that you can learn the secret of the Maine islands. For if you are lucky enough to be on such an island in such a fog, and if you sit quietly beneath a tall, blue-green spruce, the wind will whisper through the boughs and tell you the story of the fog maiden's necklace.

In the early time, when the spirits of land, sea, and sky had human forms, there was a beautiful maiden of fog. Often, the fog maiden would put on her dress and veil of gray mist, brush her long hair until it gleamed like softly burnished silver, and visit her brother, the sea, and her mother, the land.

Wherever she went, the fog maiden always wore her most precious possession, an intricate seashell necklace. In all the world there was no necklace like the fog maiden's; it was made of all the shells the sea could create. There were pearly white barnacles and violet blue mussels; even the small, speckled limpets had a place. But what the fog maiden loved most about the necklace was that all the colors of the rainbow sparkled in its shells.

One day, when the fog maiden was visiting her brother the sea, she saw a young fisherman pulling in his nets. He had black hair and sparkling green eyes the color of pine trees, and the fog maiden loved him with her whole heart.

But knowing that a spirit could never marry a mortal, she visited her sister the birch, who was very wise.

"How can I become a mortal maiden, so that I might marry the young fisherman?" asked the fog maiden.

"There is only one way," answered the birch in her wisest voice. "You must give your necklace back to the sea."

The fog maiden looked sadly down at her necklace. Its rainbow hues of pink and lavender shone as the sun peeked through the arms of the birch. "Surely," she pleaded, "there is another way."

"No, little sister," said the birch. "You carry all the magic of the sea, for good or for harm, in your necklace, and to become mortal, you must forsake that power."

"I will keep my necklace one more day," said the fog maiden finally. "Tomorrow, I will surely give it up gladly."

And as she went on her way, the birch whispered, "Tomorrow . . ."

But when tomorrow came, the necklace seemed even more beautiful than before, and although the fog maiden watched the young fisherman day after day and thought that her heart would break without him, she could not give her necklace back to the sea.

Then one day, the north wind and the sea began to argue about who was the stronger. They were soon tossing wildly in a fight. The fog maiden watched, terrified, as the young fisherman's boat was buffeted between the wind and the sea. The north wind swiped angrily at the sea, the sea lunged at the wind. Then the small boat overturned, and the fisherman was swept far out to sea.

He will perish, thought the fog maiden in despair. Then she held her necklace to her ear and listened carefully. A gentle voice was calling to her through the roar of wind and sea.

". . . all the magic of the sea, for good or for harm . . ."

The fog maiden knew what she must do. She took one last look at her beautiful seashell necklace, swiftly broke the strand that held it together, and watched the rainbow-colored shells dance to the sea.

As each shell touched the water, it became a bit of land until the sea was a patchwork of islands large and small.

The young fisherman had just enough strength to swim to the nearest of these islands. He lay there, exhausted, for a long while. Then, looking up, he saw a maiden with soft, gray eyes and mist in her hair. The fisherman loved the maiden at once. They were married that very day and made their home on that very island.

There they lived many long and happy years. Being a simple

man, the fisherman never did ask his wife where she had come from. But on days when the north wind blew a veil of fog across their island, he always brought a bunch of many-colored wildflowers home for his wife.

Taking the flowers, she would laugh happily, and her gray eyes would brighten. "Here they are," she would say, "all the colors of the rainbow!"

Geraldine Marshall Gutfreund *has published five books for children and more than fifty stories, articles, and poems for children and adults. She and her husband have two daughters, a dachshund dog, and a cat.*

Aye! no monuments

RITA JOE

Ai! Mu knu´kaqann,
Mu nuji-wi´kikaqann,
Mu weskitaqawikasinukl kisna
   mikekni-napuikasinukl
Kekinua´tuenukl wlakue´l
   pa´qalaiwaqann.

Ta´n teluji-mtua´lukwi´tij nuji-
kina´mua´tijik a.

Ke´kwilmi´tij,
Maqamikewe´l wisunn,
Apaqte´l wisunn,
Sipu´l;
Mukk kasa´tu mikuite´tmaqanmk
Wula knu´kaqann.

Ki´kelu´lk nemitmikl
Kmtne´l samqwann nisitk,
Kesikawitkl sipu´l.
Wula na kis-napui´kmu´kl
Mikuite´tmaqanminaq.

Nuji-kina´masultioq.
  we´jitutoqsip ta´n kisite´mekl

Wisunn aqq ta´n pa´qi-klu´lk,
Tepqatmi´tij Lnu weja´tekemk
  weji-nsituita´timk.

Aye! no monuments,
No literature,
No scrolls or canvas-drawn pictures
Relate the wonders of our yesterday.
How frustrated the searchings
  of the educators.

Let them find
Land names,
Titles of seas,
Rivers;
Wipe them not from memory.
These are our monuments.

Breathtaking views—
Waterfalls on a mountain,
Fast flowing rivers.
These are our sketches
Committed to our memory.
Scholars, you will find our art
In names and scenery,
Betrothed to the Indian
  since time began.

Rita Joe *lives in Eskasoni, Nova Scotia. She has published many of her poems and records of Micmac legends in the* Micmac News *and in* Bluenose Magazine. We Are the Dreamers *is her latest book.*

A Wild, Rank Place

HENRY DAVID THOREAU

Between 1849 and 1855, Henry David Thoreau took several trips to Cape Cod and wrote a book by that name that described what he found there. Today most people associate Cape Cod's beaches with scenic beauty and recreation. But the following excerpt reveals the raw and sometimes grisly side of the seashore in the nineteenth century.

It was even more cold and windy to-day than before, and we were frequently glad to take shelter behind a sand-hill. None of the elements were resting. On the beach there is a ceaseless activity, always something going on, in storm and in calm, winter and summer, night and day. Even the sedentary man here enjoys a breadth of view which is almost equivalent to motion. In clear weather the laziest may look across the Bay as far as Plymouth at a glance, or over the Atlantic as far as human vision reaches, merely raising his eyelids; or if he is too lazy to look after all, he can hardly help *hearing* the ceaseless dash and roar of the breakers. The restless ocean may at any moment cast up a whale or a wrecked vessel at your feet. All the reporters in the world, the most rapid stenographers, could not report the news it brings. No creature could move slowly where there was so much life around. The few wreckers were either going or coming, and the ships and the sand-pipers, and the screaming gulls overhead; nothing stood still but the shore. The little beach-birds trotted past close to the water's edge, or paused but an instant to swallow their food, keeping time with the elements. I wondered how they ever got used to the sea, that they ventured so near the waves. Such tiny inhabitants the land brought forth! except one fox. And what could a fox do, looking on the Atlantic from that high bank? What is the sea to a fox? Sometimes we met a wrecker with his cart and dog,—and his dog's faint bark at us wayfarers, heard through the roaring surf, sounded ridiculously faint. To see a little trembling dainty-footed cur stand on the margin of the ocean, and ineffectually bark at a beach-bird, amid the roar of the Atlantic! Come with design to bark at a whale, perchance! That sound will do for farmyards. All the dogs looked out of place there, naked and as if shuddering at the vastness; and I thought that they would not have been there had it not been for the countenance of their masters. Still less could you think of a cat bending her steps that way, and shaking her wet foot over the Atlantic; yet even this happens sometimes, they tell me. In summer I saw the tender young of the Piping Plover, like chickens just hatched, mere pinches of down on two legs, running in troops, with a faint peep, along the edge of the waves. I used to see packs of half-wild dogs haunting the lonely beach on the south shore of Staten Island, in New York Bay, for the sake of the carrion there cast up; and I remember that once, when for a long time I had heard a furious barking in the tall grass of the marsh, a pack of half a dozen large dogs burst forth on to the beach, pursuing a little one which ran straight to me for protection, and I afforded it with some stones, though at some risk to myself; but the next day the little one was the first to bark at me. . . .

Sometimes, when I was approaching the carcass of a horse or ox which lay on the beach there, where there was no living creature in sight, a dog would unexpectedly emerge from it and slink away with a mouthful of offal.

The sea-shore is a sort of a neutral ground, a most advantageous point from which to contemplate this world. It is even a trivial place. The waves forever rolling to the land are too far-travelled and untamable to be familiar. Creeping along the endless beach amid the sun-squall and the foam, it occurs to us that we, too, are the product of sea-slime.

It is a wild, rank place, and there is no flattery in it. Strewn with crabs, horse-shoes, and razor-clams, and whatever the sea casts up,—a vast *morgue,* where famished dogs may range in packs, and crows come daily to glean the pittance which the tide leaves them. The carcasses of men and beasts together lie stately up upon its shelf, rotting and bleaching in the sun and waves, and each tide turns them in their beds, and tucks fresh sand under them. There is naked Nature, inhumanly sincere, wasting no thought on man, nibbling at the cliffy shore where gulls wheel amid the spray.

Henry David Thoreau *was born in Massachusetts in 1817 and devoted much of his life to the observation and celebration of the natural world. He is best known as the author of* Walden: or, Life in the Woods, *and "Civil Disobedience."*

Haiku, Spring Lake, New Jersey

PENNY HARTER

twilight fading
into dark, the sea foam
brightens

full moon—
from wave to wave
the same

moon wet beach—
where the wave recedes,
sandpipers

in back of
the fish market, buckets
of the summer moon

meteor shower—
the glimmer
of the surf

in her dream
grandmother arranges
seashells

Penny Harter *taught for many years in the New Jersey Poets-in-the-Schools program. She now teaches seventh and ninth grades at Santa Fe Preparatory School.*

The Great Marsh

JENNIFER ACKERMAN

According to the author, the marsh described here was created seven thousand years ago when rising ocean waters turned a valley of the Broadkill River into a small lagoon. Over time, the lagoon grew clogged with silt, which provided a foothold for grasses, which trapped soil in their roots to make the marsh.

Just before sunrise, low tide. I walk out into the marsh in the dark, stepping around chocolate brown pools agitated with the scratching and scuttling of fiddler crabs, past delicate marsh pinks, absent their color in the white-wash light. Waves of warm air waft up from the mudbanks bared by the outcreeping tide, a strong sulphur smell, not unpleasant. The beam of my flashlight catches the giant ghostly pale blossoms of the seashore mallow, *Kosteletzkya virginica*. I linger here for a moment, hoping to "shine" the eyes of a wolf spider, a species with mirrorlike membranes that reflect light.

The darkness of the marsh is not the close darkness of woods, where blackness pours up from between the trees, but a thin, liquid, open, far-reaching darkness that descends onto the grass. Silence stretches from horizon to horizon, broken only by the occasional call of a whippoorwill, a sound that carries easily over the flat topography, somehow amplified by the open acres of air and the drum-flat surface of the nearby bay. . . .

Pull up the blanket of marsh, give it a shake, and out would tumble coffee-bean snails, *Melampus bidentatus,* little half-inch creatures tinted with brown and green, as well as grasshoppers, beetles, ants, flies, and cinch bugs, which feed on *Spartina's* tender leaves, and plant hoppers, which suck its juices. Also fiddler crabs and mud crabs, oysters and dense clumps of ribbed mussels, which pave the mud along the creeks where the tide floods regularly. According to one study, this marsh supports more than three and a half million mussels per acre. Out, too, would tumble diamondback terrapins, turtles the size of a small skull, their segmented pentagons fused to form a leathery dome, their reptilian heads spotted like a leopard. The diamondback was once here in great numbers, but its sweet flesh made it a gastronomic delicacy and the target of tireless collectors.

The shake wouldn't loose such tenacious insiders as the larva of the common marsh fly, family Chloropidae, which lives in the stems of *Spartina* and eats the plant's tissue. (The adults are so small, only two or three millimeters long, that they are nearly invisible except when swarming.) Nor would it dislodge the larvae of the fierce-biting greenhead fly, whose singular appetites are described by John and Mildred Teal in *Life and Death of the Salt Marsh.* "The larvae are maggots, soft, elongate, leathery-skinned, lumpy individuals with a pair of organs for breathing air at one end and a pair of sharp jaws at the other. They wriggle through the mud eating anything they come across, including others of their kind. If a number of *Tabanus* maggots are put together in a dish, the end result is one fat, temporarily contented individual."

Here are some of the thirty or so species of fish that swim the waters of the Great Marsh: the small, glistening fish known as silversides, the four-spined stickleback, anchovy, northern pipefish, two kinds of herring, young striped bass, sea robins, summer flounder, naked gobies, striped mullet and white perch, eel, croaker, menhaden, northern kingfish, and three species of killifish, including the mummichog, a name that comes from a Narraganset word meaning "they go in great numbers."

The sun has reappeared above the cloud reef, a second bloom. In this low morning light the marsh looks different than it does under cloud cover or high sun, not a hazy watercolor wash, but a dazzling mosaic of distinctly different greens. The tide is sliding up the marsh slope, slithering into the creeks and spilling over between the blades of grass. The up, down, in, out of the tides makes this place dangerous—sometimes inundating animals with lethal doses of saltwater, sometimes exposing them to a devastating high-and-dry death—but also inconceivably rich. The tides distribute food and flush out waste, encouraging rapid growth and quick decay. Adaptation to this pulse is the contract that all successful marsh creatures have signed with a country half land, half sea. When the ebbing tide bares the flats, hundreds of scraping chitinous legs and claws scribe the mud as fiddler crabs emerge from their burrows to search for bacteria, fungi, minute algae, and fermenting marsh plants. Tiny star-shaped pigment cells dotting the crab's body obey the compounded rhythms of sun and tide. The cells contain granules of dark pigment, which disperse at daytime low tide, giving the crabs the color of the mudbank and thus protecting them from predators. At night the pigment granules shrink from the cell's reaches and cluster together, the color fades, and the crabs turn the pale ivory-white of moonlight. These changes occur every day at a different hour, synchronized with the tides.

Now, as the salt tide seeps up the mudbank, the fiddlers are waiting until the water reaches their knees before they disappear into their deep mud tunnels to wait out the deluge. Though they breathe air with a primitive lung beneath the edge of their shell, they can hole up in their burrows with no oxygen for long periods—for months in cold water—a feat that makes the limit of our own tolerance for organic variation seem narrow indeed. A few moments' loss of oxygen and we rapidly descend into unconsciousness.

Coffee-bean snails, too, are air-breathers, but they go up rather than down when the tide rises. Like ghost crabs and beach fleas, they are members of a race that is learning to live outside the sea. Somehow they anticipate rising tides, creeping up the stalks of grass well before the water arrives. They take a breath of air that will hold them for an hour or so if the drowning sea submerges them.

Spiders and insects such as grasshoppers keep company with the snail, scaling stems to escape the high tide. This habit exposes the climbers to the keen eyes and hungry beaks of birds. The Teals once described the scene of an especially high tide, insects hopping, jumping, and flying onto taller plants until "only the tallest grasses along the creeks mark the meandering channels and these grasses are weighted and bending at the tips, alive with insects. Sparrows and wrens from the marsh, buntings and warblers from the land, gulls and terns from the beach, and swallows, dip, fly, settle, and swim along the twisting lanes of helpless insects and gorge themselves." I've seen swallows swooping over the marsh, snatching insects from mid-air, then suddenly dodging a marsh hawk's hook and talon in a startling turnabout of predator and prey.

Sunlight to marsh grass to grasshopper to swallow to hawk: these are some of the links that compose the marsh web. Learning a place is like this, glimpsing the individuals, the pinpoint touches of color on the broad canvas, randomly splattered. You pick them out, sort them out, name them, then tumble them back into the landscape, and by reading and more observation, figure out how they fit together. As more spaces are filled in, the image or weave is revealed, the continuous meshing intimacy. It helps to have a native tutor, and a sense of the storyline, the narrative over time. In the marsh, the little rhythms of the day have a way of focusing attention on particular species, the way the slow, small meter of an Emily Dickinson poem brings each syllable into close-up.

Jennifer Ackerman *is a writer who specializes in natural history and the biological sciences.*

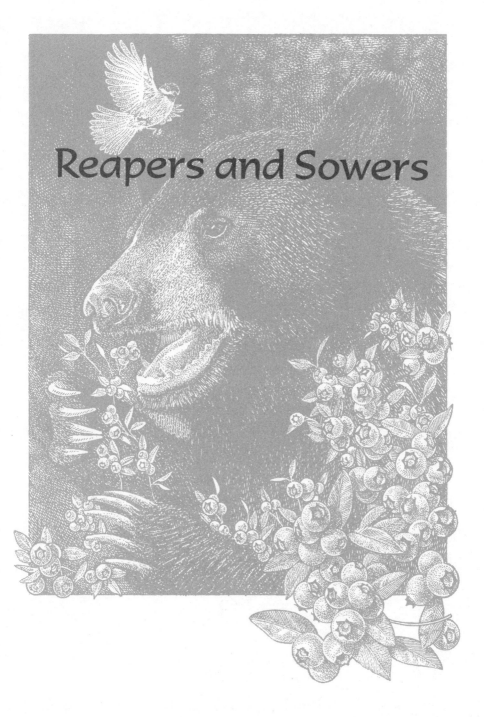

Reapers and Sowers

Blueberries

JIM GORMAN

Blueberries are a favorite food of bears, birds, and humans alike. They grow on heathlands and meadows along the North Atlantic Coast, and on blueberry farms, such as the one in this story.

It is August, and we know like birds where to find the ripe berries. We have come down Route 1 in Uncle Larry's old school bus, across the border into America, into the great state of Maine, where we used to live, Grammaw says, ninety years ago.

We are from the Micmac tribe, living in Nova Scotia now, twenty-eight of us on the bus, eleven adults not counting Grammaw, and the rest of us kids, mostly boys, but also Sister and me, two girls who have proven ourselves before, pickers with fast hands. "Twenty-eight sore backs tonight," says Uncle Larry. "Twenty-eight sore backs and fifty-six blue hands."

We arrive long before noon and are greeted by Mrs. Gable. Now it is her land, two hundred acres that slope toward the ocean. We have picked for her family for many years. She knows us, knows some of us by name.

I help Grammaw from the bus, and Mrs. Gable says, "All the rain has made them bigger this year, Grammaw. Bigger and juicier. It is a good year."

Grammaw puts out her hand and says, "It is a good year to be alive." Though she is losing her sight, she knows how to find the sun, the east, also the direction of the warm wind. She bows and says, "I can smell the ripeness. This year even the bears will not be hungry."

We join the other rakers on the barrens, a rocky plain with poor soil, limestone worn away to fine gravel. The blueberry thrives in it. The low bushes hug the ground, twisted in with weeds and prickers. You can kneel, you can crouch, or you can bend from the waist. Whatever way, a pain comes and lives in your back for all the days you are here.

Uncle Larry passes out the rakes. They look like dustpans or flour scoops, tin boxes with long tines. You face uphill and jab at the bushes with short strokes. You gather both berry and chaff as fast as you can, filling the buckets.

"Eight cents," Uncle Larry calls out. "Eight cents a pound this season. That's a good wage. I want to see some ten-dollar-a-day rakers."

Grammaw sits on a rock as we rake. The wind from the ocean lifts her thin hair. She should not have come this year. Both her body and her mind lean toward death. She counts with doubt and sometimes with bitterness each day she has outlived her daughter, our mother, who died in the winter last year. Some days Grammaw is not in this world of automobiles and electricity anymore, but drifts, sometimes here, sometimes in the world of long ago. She sits on the rock and talks again and again of Glooskap, the magic spirit, who has made all the animals and plants, made them useful to people.

The magic spirit, she says, gave us the blueberry rake, gave it first to the bear as a paw. Our people watched the bear, his powerful arm and long claws, then made their first rakes out of wood and bone, then gave both berry and rake to the white man.

But the white man has forgotten Glooskap, Grammaw says. The white man kills the bear. The white man passes his hands across the barrens and says, I own.

Grammaw says, "Only the white man needs to rake so many pounds, needs to feed so many mouths in his vast nation."

Uncle Larry speaks against her. They are like two ravens, and the rest of us smile at their squawking. Sister especially, who goes further than smiles, moving her lips with their speeches, mocking them both with her eyes. She gets the boys to watch her. She is fourteen and easy to watch if you are a boy. I give her that look that Mother used to give her—Mother's pained face, Sister calls it—and she sticks out her tongue at me, her little sister, Mama's good girl.

The voices go on above us. "The white man pays well for the food that goes into his belly," Uncle Larry says.

"But the berries will run out, nephew, some day, both the berries and our people to pick them," Grammaw says.

"But they've made new bushes now that stand up high as your chest, Grammaw. They grow in any soil with berries big as grapes," he says.

"And as sour," she says. "Sour and without the healing magic."

The hours pass. I rake my bucket full several times. Filled, it weighs about twenty pounds: $1.60, three times, four times. Uncle Larry keeps a tally, and I am high on his list.

At sundown, he and the other men set up the tents. They are not teepees, but made of nylon, bright yellow and green. The Gable family has built new showers near the fields. They are proud, showing us, and we will use them someday, Uncle Larry says politely, but tonight we ride in the bus the seven miles to the ocean. I leap into the icy waves with a shriek, and the pain goes out of my back.

Almost. I lie in the tent while the others eat. At long last Sister returns, tossing the package from the store on the blanket next to me. "Uncle Larry drove me over," she says, "just the two of us in that stupid, rattling bus. I told him we needed magazines, and he bought my little story." She snaps her chewing gum as she talks and then blows a pink bubble, a broad-faced girl who seems to have no feelings, no low spots, no holes. "He bought the magazines too, and lucky he did. You could spend a day's picking on two magazines."

Sister gives me the pills and a drink, then breaks the cellophane and hands me a scented packet. "Cheer up, girly," she says. "Every girl gets surprised her first time. I did. But Uncle Larry doesn't know, and none of the boys do either—unless I tell them." Then she lies on the other blanket, a magazine open, flipping through pages of glossy models, touching their cheeks, their lips, with her blue fingers.

Grammaw does know. But when she comes to the tent, Sister is not there but gone, out with the boys. Grammaw crouches by me and says, "Your pain is not from the picking, is it, girl?" She has a cup of steaming water, and into it she drops what look like bits of dried blood. "Blueberry tea," she says. "Not this year's berries, but ones you save. This is better than mint for your pains." Her hands are warm and moist from the hot cup. She touches my forehead and then rubs my temples. Pulse to pulse I feel the blood in her fingers. I lean my head into her and say, "Rock me," and she does, whispering, "Your mammaw is still here, isn't she, in this wide brow of yours, and in how you work without resting. This day you raked with the fast hands of a child. This night you have the pains of a woman."

Jim Gorman *has published two chapbooks of stories and won an Ohio Arts Council Individual Artist Fellowship in fiction writing in 1996. He teaches at Otterbein College in Ohio and coordinates the Otterbein Community Poetry Workshop, which brings college students together with at-risk youth.*

Pauline Sings across the Rooftops

Julie Parson-Nesbitt

Summer bees, their soft voices
the sweet packages their legs carry
Pauline sings.

Falling leaf, wind in branches
nest apple the wind buries
Pauline sings:

Brother, brother, bumblebee
pirate sailor come to me
sail across our mother water
with gifts of gold and sandbox treasure.

Crocus bulb, cradle ember
firethorn and baby's thimble
quiet steps the street remembers
bagpipes calling dreams to waking
fly like flags across the rooftops
Pauline sings.

From your dream of windy bridges
tell us, tell us
in your subway lullaby

---

how you found us. We think you followed
snow falling through plane trees. We heard
you hopscotched here on sidewalk slate
to sky blue, turn around, turn around child
pebbles in your fingers,
turn around, turn around child.
Tell us the secret to pick up sticks so carefully
so the walls won't come tumbling down
tumbling tumbling down.

Sparrow-elf, cricket sister
we will bring you every pleasure:
blue balloons and yellow feathers
October moons and lady slippers.
Cry Pauline, we'll feed your hungers
we'll hang your crib with rainy roses
cry, cricket, cry.

Crocus bulb, cradle ember
you will bring us every pleasure
firethorn and wind in branches
quiet steps the street remembers
with your heart a fingered steeple
playground filled with children swinging
bagpipes calling dreams to waking
fly like flags across the rooftops

Pauline sings.

Julie Parson-Nesbitt *has received the Gwendolyn Brooks Poetry Award and two Academy of American Poets awards. Her poetry collection is* Finders *(West End Press). A Chicago writer, she has worked as a poet-in-the-schools and is executive director of the Guild Complex, a literary organization.*

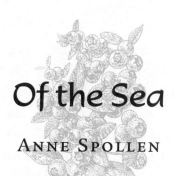

Of the Sea

ANNE SPOLLEN

This story is based on a real person Anne Spollen knew as a child while living along Raritan Bay in Staten Island, New York.

The house on the Atlantic harbor beach was tiny—a shack, really—slanting to one side with shining bald patches on its exterior where decades of wind had detached shingles. Beneath the shingles lay speckled tar paper that glistened when sun touched the house. On a sunny day, motes of light combined with the surrounding seascape to give the shack an enchanted air, as if deep within its dank swell of wood there existed a kind of magic.

I had always wondered about the shack's owner. My parents told me he was a fisherman named Duke. That explained why I rarely saw him: fishermen rose before dawn to gather their day's catch. By the time he returned home, I had already left for school. I had seen him a few times during the summer, but we had never spoken. I longed to meet him and see the interior of his cottage.

One week in late summer, two unusual events occurred: we had six straight days of rain; and Monsey Rose, a cousin I had never met from upstate New York, came to stay with us. Monsey and I were almost the same age, and we liked each other right away. The day after she arrived, the weather cleared and we were able to venture outside.

We lived about a quarter mile up from the beach. Between our house and the sand lay a patch of marsh. Normally, the marshland consisted only of damp soil visited by a variety of birds. But now the constant rain had swollen its arteries to the point that Monsey Rose and I could paddle a rowboat through the cattails, down to the hem of the bay.

"Where I live, all we have is a reservoir," Monsey Rose said. "And no one is allowed to swim there."

"Then have you ever seen anything like this?" I asked, pointing over the side of the boat.

Monsey Rose turned to see the water at low tide, exposing a rich garden of mollusk, kelp, and sea grass. A squadron of gulls squalled, diving into the seabed in search of food. We stopped to watch the gulls for a moment.

"How can gulls stay in the air without flapping their wings?" Monsey asked.

"They're gliding on the wind," I told her. "I think they're graceful, don't you?"

Monsey nodded. We got out of the rowboat and lashed its bow to a log. Then we waded the last few feet to the sandy beach.

"What on earth is that?" Monsey asked, pointing to a horseshoe crab scuttling back from shore toward the water.

"It's one of these," I said. I picked up a dead horseshoe crab and turned it onto its back. With its undersides exposed, double rows of short, meaty claws hooked the air. "My dad says they haven't changed since prehistoric times."

"You mean they looked just like this to the dinosaurs?"

I nodded.

"We have nothing like this up where I live in Taconic Park," Monsey said. "Thank goodness."

We walked into the warm, fishy wind. At last we stood by Duke's cottage.

"Who lives here?" Monsey asked. "It's such a tiny house."

"A fisherman," I answered. "I only know his name is Duke."

"So you've never met him?"

"Never."

"Or seen the inside of his house?" Monsey asked.

"No, never."

"Do you suppose he's home now?" Monsey smiled slyly as she asked this.

I looked over to the side of his house where he usually tied his boat to a piling. It was gone.

"He must be out in the bay." I quickly scanned the water for any sight of his skiff, but he was evidently still far from shore.

"Do you think he'd mind if we just peeked around his yard a bit?" Monsey asked.

"Well . . . ," I stammered. I had always wanted to get a closer look at the cottage, but I feared that Duke would get back in time to catch us.

"Oh, c'mon, just for a minute," Monsey urged. She rounded the corner into Duke's yard.

I followed Monsey, still glancing over my shoulder for any sign of Duke. But once I saw his yard, I forgot to look back. "A garden!" I exclaimed. "Look at this, Monsey!"

Before us spread neat rows, alive with bursts of flowers, tomatoes, peppers, beans, and ruffles of edible greens as borders. "My mother has been trying to grow flowers in this sandy soil for years and she's never had any kind of luck. I wonder how he grew this garden on the beach."

"I don't know," Monsey said. "But
look at this!" She held a large, dried crab
shell filled with powder that looked like salt.
"There are tiny pieces of bone in here!"

"Bones?" I peered inside the shell. "Are you sure?"

Monsey shrugged and put the shell down. "That's what
it looks like to me. And look—here's a knife!"

She picked up the strangest looking knife I had ever seen.
Several clamshells had been whittled down, then glued to a
stick. The knife was large and looked dangerously sharp.

"This place is beginning to give me the creeps," I said.

"I just want to take one quick peek inside," Monsey said.
"Are you sure he's not coming?"

I took another look at the bay. I saw a boat coming toward
shore, but it was smaller than Duke's.

Monsey tiptoed over to Duke's window and cupped her hands around her eyes. "Is he married?" she called out.

"Not that I know of," I answered. "Why?"

"Come look," she said.

I walked over to the window and peered in next to Monsey. A painted and framed portrait of a young woman hung on the wall over the kitchen table. Beneath her Duke had placed a table setting, as if the young woman were about to step down from the painting and dine with him.

"What do you think is going on there?" I asked.

"Something really weird," Monsey said. "I'm ready to go back to the house. Are you?"

"Yes," I answered. I stepped away from the window and something pierced my toe. "Ouch!" I yelled, pulling my foot out of my sandal. A small puncture mark was clearly visible on my big toe.

"Are you okay?" Monsey asked.

"Yes, I'm fine." Carefully, I brushed sand from the area beneath me. I pulled at a smooth piece of bone, and up from the sand came a hinged jaw with two triangular teeth still embedded in the lower half. "This is what got me."

"That looks like a shark's jaw," Monsey said in disbelief.

I nodded. "Just think—I was bitten by a shark, and all I said was 'ouch!'"

"Let's go," Monsey said. "I've seen enough for one day."

"Me, too."

We were just about to turn the corner when we saw the shadow of a figure coming toward us. I wheeled around quickly. There, lashed to the piling, was Duke's boat. That must have been his boat on the bay after all. In the distance, the craft had looked smaller.

"Hurry, this way!" I whispered.

Monsey and I scampered down a sandy knoll to our boat and paddled back to the house as quickly as we could.

"I hope you girls didn't disturb any of that man's hard work," my mother said when we told her about the things we had found in Duke's garden. "And I'm sure there's a perfectly good explanation for everything else. In fact, I'd like to see this garden." She sighed, and I knew she was thinking about her most recently failed flower bed.

The following afternoon, when we were sure Duke would be home, my mother packed a batch of brownies. We walked the length of the cove to Duke's cottage.

"You girls are unusually quiet today," my mother remarked.

Monsey and I exchanged quick glances. Before we could answer, Duke waved from his garden. "Hello there!" he called.

"Hello," my mother said. "I'm Adele Ross."

"Yes," Duke said, "I know you. And I know this one," he said, looking directly at me. "You two live just up the street from the cove. In the gray house. But this young lady . . ."

"My cousin, Monsey Rose," I said.

I did not mean to stare, but the man standing before us appeared ancient, as if his skin were made of papyrus. His hooded eyelids were wrinkled and puckered as walnut shells.

"You were the girls I saw going down into the marsh yesterday. I meant to thank you for finding my chum grinder." In his hand was the jawbone. "This was a gift from a friend who does deep sea fishing."

"Are there sharks around here?" Monsey asked.

"Oh, not here. Way out in the sea."

Monsey looked relieved.

"What's a chum grinder?" I asked.

"Here, I'll show you." Duke placed a fish carcass over the lower jaw, then dragged the fish across the teeth. The fish shredded almost instantly. "See, now I have chum—ground-up fish that attracts fluke for my catch."

"Well, we brought something more appetizing than chum," my mother said as she offered the brownies to Duke. He smiled as he accepted the plate. "I hope you don't mind, but the girls described your garden. I was wondering how anything grows in this sandy soil."

"I enrich it with treasures from the sea," Duke replied. "I've spent years mixing seaweed, fish remains, soil, and even my kitchen scraps to make gold for this garden. The mixture changes the soil so I can grow almost anything in this little patch. And here," Duke picked up the shell containing the salty powder, "I grind the fluke bones and spread the powder on the soil."

We walked around the garden. He was right about using everything from the sea. He had lashed together horseshoe crab tails as stakes for his tomato and bean vines. Herbs grew between propeller blades. A thick crust of dried seaweed lay beneath his plants to fertilize his vegetables and keep weeds from taking root.

"I can show you how to layer the compost," Duke said to my mother. "If you girls could go inside for some plates and forks, I'd be willing to share these brownies. You can bring them right out here." He gestured to a picnic table he had crafted out of driftwood.

The first thing that struck me as I entered Duke's house

was the smell: fresh and salty at the same time, like the waters of the Atlantic. "You know, Monsey, it's almost like being in the ocean when you're inside here."

"That's because he's practically brought the ocean in here," she said. I walked over to where Monsey stood in the kitchen. Duke had separated his fishing lures and weights into different-sized clamshells. All of them were shelved on planks he had made out of driftwood. Knives, forks, and spoons were neatly housed in cleaned-out hulls of horseshoe crabs. "I hope he really cleaned those things," Monsey said.

He had. In fact, he had put a clear glaze of shellac over them. I looked around at the tiny house—just a main room, a kitchen, and a small bathroom—and almost wished we had a cottage like this on the ocean. Then I looked above the small table at the haunting portrait of the young woman.

We did not see Duke and my mother standing in the doorway. Duke held a watermelon he had just picked from his garden.

"That's my wife, girls. When I eat, I get lonesome for somebody. I talk to her picture like she's still here. She died not long after we got married. She was only twenty-three." Duke looked sad for a moment. Then he added, "Clara's body may not be here, but her spirit is with me always. Right here," he said, patting his chest over his heart.

"That's a lovely thought," my mother said.

Duke sighed. Then he leaned down and opened a kitchen drawer. He took out a knife just like the one Monsey had found in the yard. We watched as he deftly sliced through the watermelon.

We ate on Duke's picnic table, looking at the ocean. "You know, I don't own a television," Duke said as he gazed into the

bay. "I watch changes in the face of the sea for entertainment."
As orange fingers of sun rippled the surface of the water, we
could see what he meant. When we finished our watermelon,
Duke politely collected all our seeds and rinds for his compost
pile.

"Well, thank you for showing me how to build a compost
pile," my mother said.

"And thank you for the delicious watermelon," Monsey
and I added.

"Thank you for the brownies," Duke said. "Come back
anytime."

And we did go back, many times.

My mother began her compost pile the day of our first visit,
assigning Monsey and me the task of gathering seaweed and a
variety of shells and rocks that she used for decoration, borders, and soil enrichment. By the following summer, for the
first time, Mother had beds of vibrant flowers.

Anne Spollen *holds an M.A. in English literature and has taught*
middle school for the past decade.

Shells

WALLY SWIST

As she taught the alphabet,
my mother collected shells,
mounting polished conchs,
augers, sundials, and whelk
in a glass case on velvet.

As a child, I recited the alphabet
as waves rolled from the sea to land.
I have never lost the words
found in a harbor, the shells
brought home from the beach.

I still pocket them
as I walk the shore
and press some to my ear
so that I can listen again
to the beginning.

Wally Swist's *books of poetry include* The New Life *(Plinth Books, 1998) and* Veils of the Divine *(Hanover Press, 2001). His poems appear in such magazines as* Appalachia, Puckerbush Review, *and* Yankee. *He is a recipient of a fellowship from the Connecticut Commission on the Arts.*

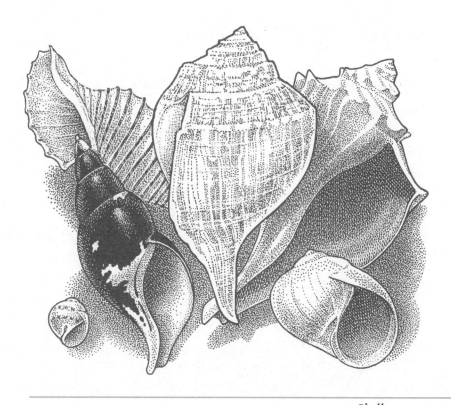

The Maize Doll

BETSY McCULLY COOPER

The place we call New York City has undergone many changes over the last four hundred years. This story takes us back to a time when New York was the home of the Lenape Indians, and gives us a glimpse of its transition to a burgeoning Dutch colony.

Lenapehoking: 1609, European time

It was the time of the Hunger, when the maize withered on the stalks and the earth became parched. One day a little girl found a stick that looked like a person, but when she brought it home, her parents shook their heads and told her to throw it away because it might be a bad spirit. The girl did as she was told and soon after fell into a fever. One night while she was ill, she dreamed that a shriveled old woman spoke to her to tell her that she must dress the stick and hold a dance and feast to honor Maize Maiden. Only in this way would Maize Maiden return and bless their crops. The next morning the girl got up and retrieved the stick, dressing it in maize husks to make a doll. Then the women and girls performed a dance. Sure enough, Maize Maiden returned, bringing with her the rains that watered the earth. The maize sprang up, and the people's health returned. In thanks, the people perform the Doll Dance every spring.

Having finished her tale, Old Story Woman sat silent, the

firelight flickering on her creased brown face and dancing in the dark pupils of her eyes. Her story sticks were arranged on the ground in the shapes of a doll and a maize stalk. The children seated around her in the Story Circle were caught in the spell of her story, Listening Girl most of all because she loved listening to stories. When a low rustling sound seemed to arise out of the shadows, the children shivered—until they saw Old Story Woman's hand emerge from under the folds of her skirt, holding a doll dressed in a cornhusk skirt: it was Ohtas, the Doll Being. Smiling, Old Story Woman spoke the words she always spoke at the end. "Never forget that you are of the Turtle Clan, people of water and land, the First People of this place, Lenapehoking." She rose, breaking the Story Circle.

Listening Girl got up slowly, reluctant to leave the warmth of the fire. Grandfather North was already blowing an icy breath, painting the leaves flaming colors. Soon, at the time of Leaf-Fall, her people would pack up and move away from their summer home on the Far Point by the Great Salt Water, upland to the Place of Tall Trees.

Listening Girl looked forward to the Snow Months. All the people of her clan came together then, living in the longhouses the men had built from hickory saplings and chestnut tree bark and greeting the Time of Snows with dancing and feasting. She couldn't wait to hear the stories the elders told when they gathered around the fire during the long winter nights. She always listened closely so that she could memorize the stories and pass them on to her children. Perhaps she would even become a Storyteller like Old Story Woman. But now, she thought as she walked toward her wigwam, there was much work to do to get ready for the move. She looked up into the night sky that glittered with stars like so many campfires.

Turning her gaze to Grandfather East, she looked for the Seven Sisters that her father said were the sign of the coming frost—and sure enough, there they were, dancing.

Listening Girl lifted the flap to her wigwam and crept to her sleeping mat. That night she dreamed that a green maize stalk grew way up to the sky, so close to the sun that her tassels caught fire. Then Grandfather North blew his icy breath, turning the tassel-flames to cinders that fell to the earth like snow, and wherever they fell, cornstalks and bean vines and pumpkins sprang up. Then she saw herself dancing in the Planting Field with Old Story Woman, both raising their hands to the sky to give thanks to Uncle Sun and to Thunderbird, who brought rain.

The next morning, as soon as the sunlight stole through the smoke hole, Listening Girl's eyes flew open. She could see her breath. She held the bearskin around her as she got up and slipped into her moccasins. Already her mother was up with the baby, tending the fire. When she saw that Listening Girl was up, she ladled thick hot maize porridge from the clay pot into a wood bowl and handed it to her. Listening Girl ate in silence, watching her mother comb out her long shiny black hair and braid it, weaving a white feather into one of the braids. They called her mother White Feather because she once had a dream of a white bird who gave her a feather and told her to heal her people. This was seen as a sign of a special gift, allowing her mother to become a medicine woman. She knew the powers of all the plants, and her people came to her for herbs and roots to cure their sickness. She always carried dried roots and herbs in a medicine pouch that she hung from her beaded sash. She motioned to her daughter to come over so she could comb and braid her hair. It was then that

Listening Girl told her mother of her dream. White Feather listened intently, worried by the burning cornstalk, then reassured at the last part. "That is a good dream, daughter; it means that you will be the Maize Maiden in the Doll Dance. You must tell Old Story Woman." Then she instructed her daughter to go wash up in the stream and meet her in the Planting Field.

As soon as Listening Girl stepped outside into the crisp air, she faced the Four Directions. To the East, Uncle Sun glowed like an ember through the mist that was rising from the ground. Listening Girl greeted Uncle Sun and thanked him for his light and warmth. To the South was the shimmering blue of the Great Salt Water, whose waves crashed on the shores of Rockaway and Canarsie. A wedge of geese flew low over the water, led by their *Sakima* or Chief Goose to the land of Grandmother South. She could clearly hear their honks. To the West, just across the Narrow Water, rose the green back of the island *Aquehonga,* place of high sandy banks, where her mother's kin lived. Beyond *Aquehonga* were the lands of the Raritan and Hackensack. To the North was *Mahicannituk,* the River That Flowed Both Ways.

She rejoiced in the beauty of her home—place of water and sky and many islands. Her village was set on a bluff overlooking the bay. Below was *Mocuny,* the low muddy place, where grasses taller than she rippled in the sea breezes. The reeds were no longer green, but now tan as deer hide. Atop a cattail, Wren sang his gurgly song. Bittern boomed loudly from her hiding place, "Gloong-KA-glunk! Gloong-KA-glunk!" The sea of grass was broken by several clearings Muskrat had made when he cut cattails and reeds to build his underwater wigwam. She could see the domed tops of the muskrat wigwams sticking up here and there in the water. At the water's edge, White Heron stood on one leg, her head cocked as she watched intently for killifish swimming in the shallows; in a blink of an eye, she extended her long neck and snapped up a fish for breakfast. Casting a shadow over the reeds, Hawk circled in the sky, hunting for his breakfast—perhaps a vole or white-footed mouse who scurried in the grasses. Listening Girl's attention was drawn by what appeared to be a whirling black cloud: it was a horde of blackbirds, ready to descend on their fields and steal their maize. Old Story Woman had taught that the Maize-Thief had brought the first grain of corn and first bean from the Creator to them, so they must respect Blackbird and not harm him.

Remembering that she must be in the Planting Field soon, she hurried to the stream, carefully picking her way along the path through the meadow so as not to step on any plants. Her mother had taught her that all plants are sacred and must be treated with respect. Soon, her mother would teach her the healing ways of plants and how to collect them. Many flowers and grasses had sprung up in the clearing her people had made here so they could build their houses and plant their fields. Goldenrods, asters, and gayfeathers brightened the meadow with their yellows and purples. She could hardly see the yellow wands of the goldenrod because they were covered with the orange-and-black wings of the Flowers-That-Fly. Other Winged Creatures browsed in the meadow flowers, buzzing and droning. The grasses and herbs were bursting with seeds, food for the little brown sparrows who flew up at her approach. She loved the songs of these birds in the spring, especially the sweet, clearly whistled notes of the one with the dark spot on its breast, singing joyfully from a tree branch.

Now the birds were silent, busily fattening up for the Snow Months.

In the soft mud of the stream bank, Listening Girl noted the tracks left by Red Fox, out hunting last night. Kneeling on the bank of the stream, she saw in its clear water schools of little silvery fish heading into the current; these were babies of the big fish who swam upstream from the Great Salt Water every spring, during the time of the Great Fish-Run. Her father and other men would cast their nets of woven reeds weighted with stones, and the fish would swim right into them. So many fish crowded the streams, her father told her, that a man could walk across the water on their backs! The shad were the first to arrive, followed by the great striped bass. The men would easily spear these fish, then split and clean and dry them over smoky fires on wooden racks they had set up on the beach. Of course, they would also bring some fresh fish home to their women to prepare, seasoning them with berries and herbs and baking them on hickory-wood planks set close to the fire.

A sudden sound of shouting broke her reverie. It was the voices of the old men and young boys who were on the beach below the bluff, where they were gathering and drying shell-fish for winter use. Listening Girl jumped up and ran back through the meadow to the edge of the bluff. She was astonished to see what appeared to be a tall straight tree trunk tipped in clouds floating on the water. Then a second and a third tall cloud-tipped tree appeared, and then a floating island like an upside-down turtle shell, growing larger and closer. "Manitou! Manitou!" she murmured. "There is a powerful spirit at work here!" Before she could run to the Planting Field to alert the women and girls, they had dropped their tools and run out to the bluff. Old Story Woman emerged from her wigwam, looking out toward the water. She gasped. Listening Girl ran up to her. "What can it mean, Old Story Woman?" she asked.

"It is the Floating-Island-of-Winds my grandmother told me about, which one morning during the Moon-of-Seed-Sowing brought strange Men-with-Hair-on-Their-Faces. When they started to come ashore in a large canoe, Thunderbird blew a great wind over the Salt Water, forcing them to turn around and return to their Floating Island." Old Story Woman scanned the sky. "Today there will be no great wind, and they will come ashore. We must greet them with plenty of food and make them feel welcome. We will see what they want, but surely they will not want to harm the First People of Lenapehoking."

New Amsterdam, fifty solar years later (650 moons) . . .

When Anna woke up that morning, she wasn't sure where she was at first, but then she remembered: she and her mother, Sara, were visiting Grandma to help her prepare for market day, when the farm women gathered to sell their produce. Although a market was held every Saturday, the harvest market was special, for then the women traveled from all parts of New Netherland, bringing their handmade linens, laces, and woolens along with their farm produce. The Indian women also came to sell their wares, and the commerce between Dutch and Wilden was always lively. Her own mother had persuaded the governor to start the weekly market on the Strand, near the dock, and had even built a shed in her backyard to house the Indian women who came for the event. Because she spoke fluent Algonkian, she often served as translator between tribal representatives and government officials or traders. Relations between Indian and Dutch could get tense, and Sara was often able to smooth things over. Her diplomatic skills and warm hospitality made her esteemed by the local Indians—even the Hackensack chief, Oratani, called her a friend.

Anna peered at her mother through the linen curtains of her wall bed. Dressed in a blue linen gown, her hair braided and coiled beneath a white linen headdress, her mother was a handsome woman. She was busily loading a basket with earthenware crocks of preserves and pickles. Another basket was piled high with the fresh apples and pears that Anna had helped pick from Grandma's orchard.

Anna loved visiting Grandma's farm. Many a happy summer day she had spent taking walks with Grandma, going berry picking or mushroom hunting or collecting wild plants. Grandma seemed to know everything about plants. "That low plant growing on the ground is plantain," she would say, "what the Wilden call White Man's Foot because it seems to spring up wherever we walk! The leaves make a poultice for burns. That tall plant there with broad leaves and a fat seed pod is called the milkweed because of its bitter milky sap; its fluffy seed tassels stuff your pillow. The sweet leaves of purple bee balm make a soothing tea, and the roots of the aster, with its starlike purple flowers, make a good tea to cool a fever. Those sunflowers you see have a thick tuber that can be boiled and eaten—an Indian food. If you know where to look in the thickets by the stream—and if you let the sweet smell of its pealike flowers guide you—you can find the groundnut vine, whose meaty root is delicious." Once Anna asked her how she knew so much about plants. Annekje told her that every good Dutch housewife must know the uses of plants, if she is to tend to her family's ailments. "I learned from my mother, but when I came to this country, I could not find the plants I knew. Of course, I brought seeds from the old country to plant in my herb garden, but it was the Wilden who taught me about the wild plants, for they know the earth like their mother." Now, Annekje—whom the townspeople called Widow Bogart—was known to Dutch and Indian alike for her skills in healing.

"Where's Grandma?" Anna asked as she swung her legs out from under her feather quilt and over the sides of the bed.

Her mother answered, "Out to gather eggs from her chickens, with no help from you! So up with you, lazy bones, and help us get to market!"

Used to her mother's good-natured scolding, she happily complied. She needed no encouragement to get up on market day! Her grandmother's maid, Trina, dished out *suppone*—corn mush mixed with buttermilk and molasses—from the iron pot that hung over the hearth and set it on the wooden table. Anna ate quickly, then stepped outside to the well, where she could wash herself with the cool water she drew up in the wooden bucket. The sun was just rising over the fields like a piece of molten iron on the blacksmith's anvil, lighting up the bay. She could see Staten Island in the distance, and beyond that the highlands of Sandy Hook. A salty breeze rippled the marsh grasses below, where cows were grazing. In the mudflats, hogs rooted for shellfish.

The clomping of horse's hoofs and clatter of wheels startled Anna out of her reverie. It was time to go to market! Once everything was loaded, they were on their way, the two women and the girl sitting atop the cart seat facing backward so they could steady the baskets, while Grandma's bond servant Peter guided the horse along the road to the ferry.

The farms receded before Anna's eyes, field after field of stubble where wheat and tobacco had been harvested. Now men were cutting hay and stacking them into bales for winter feed, or repairing fences, or ploughing where they planned to put in winter wheat. Black men and white men worked these fields; the white men were bond servants who had to serve their time as field hands and servants in exchange for ship passage to the new country, and the black men were slaves brought from Africa and the West Indies to work company plantations. A few of the slaves, Anna knew, had been granted their freedom and a plot of land where they could raise their children.

At the ferry landing, Peter unloaded the cart and placed their baskets in ferryman Dircksen's boat. There was a good breeze, so the ferryman could put up his sail instead of having to row them across to New Amsterdam. Anna could see the town easily, with its fort and windmill overlooking the North and East Rivers, the Dutch flag flapping its orange and blue colors over the fort. Among the rows of shops and houses clustered near the dock, she could pick out her own house, one of the new two-story brick houses with a red tile roof and step gable. Her father, Hans, the town doctor, needed to live in the town center so that he could serve the soldiers, sailors, and white and Indian traders who frequented the dock. They were a rough lot, given to drinking and fighting, so Anna was not allowed to go alone among them. Still, she could watch from her window the ships coming in, bearing exotic cargo: spices and silk from the East Indies, tea from China, wine from Portugal, rum and sugar and molasses from the West Indies. This cargo

would be unloaded, then the ships would take on new cargo—
the furs, lumber, sacks of grain, and cured tobacco that were
the products of the colony.

The dock was bustling with activity as men and women
milled about, speaking all kinds of languages: Dutch, English,
French, Italian, Portuguese, Algonkian dialects, and the languages of Africa. Indian agents were earnestly negotiating
with Dutch traders over the price of the furs the Indians had
brought from upriver to exchange for cloth and blankets,
metal tools, and wampum, which was Indian money made
from shell beads. Anna knew from her father—who often
treated the Indians and saw the bad effects of liquor—that
rum was often passed around to sweeten the deal, even though
this was illegal.

Anna looked forward to seeing the Indian women at their
booths because they always had a kind word for Sara's daughter and the most interesting things to sell besides. So after
helping Sara and Annekje set out their wares, she scampered
off, making her way through the crowds of excited children,
barking dogs, squawking chickens, bleating lambs, and squeal-
ing pigs; past tables piled high with colorful vegetables and
fruits, stacks of preserves and pickles, and neatly folded linen
and lace. She found the women seated cross-legged on reed
mats, dressed in dyed cloth skirts and blouses. They were older
women—those who could be spared from the tasks of the harvest—who brought many wonderful things: fine-woven hemp
baskets and bags, bayberry soaps and candles, maplewood
spoons, calabash bowls, hickory-wood fish planks, neatly tied
straw brooms, and beaded deerskin moccasins and sashes.
There were foods, too: smoked oysters and clams, dried berries, maple sugar and syrup.

Anna's attention was drawn to an old woman who sat somewhat apart from the others and was dressed in traditional deerskin garb. She had bowls of dried herbs and maize dolls. She noticed that one of the dolls was larger than the others. It was made of a long piece of polished wood, with a knob that was carved into a woman's head, long silky black hair held by a headband, a deerskin blouse, cornhusk skirt, beaded sash, and moccasins.

"Is this for sale?" asked Anna.

"No, child, I bring doll for good fortune."

"My grandma told me that the maize doll brings good crops and health, and that the Indians have a Doll Dance to honor her."

"That is so," agreed the woman, who now eyed Anna with interest. "And how did your grandma learn this?"

"She says she learned much from the Indians in the old days—about wild plants that feed and heal us."

"Is she here, child?" Anna nodded. "Bring her to me, and tell her that I am old woman with herbs to sell."

Anna hurried back to her grandmother's booth and beckoned her to come. "There is a strange old woman who wants to see you; she makes maize dolls and has herbs to sell." Annekje's face lit up with the prospect of meeting a new Indian woman who knew herbs. Together, Anna and her grandmother walked back to see the maize-doll woman. When the two old women saw each other, a shock of recognition passed between them. Both brought their hands to their hearts in show of friendship, then exchanged greetings in Algonkian. Grandma turned to Anna. "Go, child, and help your mother. I'll be here awhile. Tonight I will have a long story to tell."

True to her word, Grandma told her story after supper at Sara's house, when the family gathered before the great hearth.

When I first came to New Netherland, your mother was just a tiny child. This place would be the only home she would know, but for me, newly married to a young farmer, I would find the new land strange and hard. Here the woods grew thickly, much of the ground was hilly and stony, and the marshes extended as far as the eye could see! I missed the flat lush meadows and fields of home, our neat houses and flower gardens all fenced round. Here we had to start from scratch: to cut the trees to make our houses; to drain the marsh to make pasture for our cattle; to clear the land for our crops. At first we lived like animals in the ground, in dugouts lined with bark and sod or reeds for roofs.

We could not have survived without our Wilden friends. We learned from them how to make wigwams of saplings and bark, where we could live until our houses were finished. They gave us maize and beans, which we planted in hills without need of ploughing. They taught us how to dry wild fruits and smoke meat and fish to preserve them. And they showed us the wild plants that would nourish us and heal us in times of sickness.

It was not long after we arrived here that your mother became ill. I did not know what to do, because it was a strange illness that my herbs could not help. One day, an Indian woman about my age came to my door. She had heard about my child's trouble and had come to offer help. Her mother had taught her the healing ways, she said, and she brought her medicine pouch. I decided to trust her.

She spent many days by Sara's side, feeding her teas and broth, rubbing her skin with salves made from plants, singing and chanting. Each day, Sara got better and was soon well. I was amazed and grateful. During that time, we spoke in broken Dutch and Algonkian. I learned that her home was at Nayack, not far from where I now live. When she was a girl about your age, she saw Hudson's boat come into the bay. She told me that after the white man came, her people became very sick, as if an ill wind had followed the sails of the white man's boats. She lost her mother, father, sister, and brother, and many of her kin to the terrible sickness. The medicine men and women were unable to cure their people. Some thought that the Great Spirit was angry with them because they had become greedy for the white man's goods, so they burned everything they had—and the sickness went away. She herself left the land that had been the home of her mothers as far back as memory could go. She went to live with kin on Staten Island, and married a young trader, and bore him three children. Her husband was often away upriver hunting for furs to supply the Dutch traders. He would go away for longer and longer times because the beaver and other fur animals moved farther and farther away. Sometimes her husband came home empty-handed. Then came the time of the Indian wars.

Our people were greedy for the land and wanted to see the Indians off the land, so our governor set tribe against tribe, arming some and not others. Warriors from different tribes would fight with each other over who had the right to the fur animals. But when they realized that we wanted them off their lands forever—that they weren't just signing a deed to share land rights—enemies formed alliances and struck back. They burned our farms and villages—this happened in my time, and I well remember the fires that raged through the land and the smoke that could be seen for miles. And I will never forget how Governor Kieft— evil man that he was—ordered a surprise attack on a group of Indians who had sought refuge in New Amsterdam from their enemies—how his soldiers set upon them like wolves in the dead of night, slaughtering men, women, and children in the innocence of their sleep! When the Indian wars were over, thousands of Dutch and Indian people had died. Her husband was among the dead.

She came to me with her children and asked to stay for awhile. Of course I welcomed her—as did my husband—for we owed her our daughter's life. She made a wigwam and camped on our farm. She and her children all helped with the farm chores—because the Wilden never take something for nothing. Sara became friends with her children and began to learn Algonkian, which is why she is so fluent now. My friend taught me many of the Indian medicine plants, and I shared my knowledge in return—but I could never learn in a summer as much as she had learned in her lifetime. At the end of summer, after the harvest, she and her children left to join her kin in the Far Country. And that is the last I saw of her until today.

Anna stared wide-eyed at the fire, whose reflection danced in her eyes. The gleaming tiles arrayed around the fireplace with their Biblical scenes could not hold her attention the way her grandmother's story had. "Why has she come back?" asked Anna.

"She wishes to pay her final respects to the dead who are buried in her homeland, before she joins her daughters on their journey westward, across the mountains."

"Why won't she stay here? Some Wilden still live at Nayack."

"She cannot remain in the land of the dead. She says that the land is no longer what she knew: the great trees are cut down, the white man's animals trample woods and marsh, and the wild animals are gone. Her people can no longer walk freely across their land because the fences block their way." Now her grandmother asked Anna to get her a bundle that lay on the table. Anna rose and fetched it, curious to know what was in it. It rustled when she carried it, as if it had dried herbs in it. Her grandmother unrolled the linen and took out a maize doll. "My friend wished for you to have this. She hopes that you will remember her story, and the story of the maize doll—and that you will tell it to your children." Anna gently took the doll into her hands.

"What is she called, Grandma, so I can remember her?"

"She says they called her Listening Girl when she was your age because she loved to listen to the stories of the elders; now they call her Storytelling Woman, because she tells the story of her people wherever they go, so their children do not forget."

That night, Anna lay with her doll beside her. She thought of the old woman and imagined how the land must have looked to her as a girl. She thought of what it must feel like to lose so much that you love. Then she fell into a dream. In the dream, she was holding the hands of an old woman who sometimes looked like Grandma, and sometimes like Grandma's friend. They were walking in a field, and the woman was telling her to walk gently so as not to harm Our Mother. There were tall cornstalks in the field, green with ripening ears of corn. The old woman and the girl danced around the corn, raising their hands to the sky. Then the girl found herself flying like a bird, with all the fields and woods and marshes and waters stretched out below her—and she was filled with the green, gold, and blue beauty of this place of many islands—beauty that was not hers to keep, but to guard, the way a bird keeps its nest against harm.

Note: Although this story is fictional, it is based on many true things. The Lenape, or Delaware, people once lived along the Middle Atlantic Coast between the Delaware and Hudson Rivers, which they called Lenapehoking. Listening Girl's village was Nayack, or "Far Point," on a bluff overlooking New York Bay in what is now Fort Hamilton, Brooklyn. Annekje and Sara were real Dutch women who were known for their extensive knowledge of medicinal herbs. Annekje's farm was located in Brooklyn, and the "road to the ferry" was later to be called Fulton Street. New Amsterdam is the Dutch name for Manhattan.

Betsy McCully Cooper *is a writer and teacher who calls New York City her home. For the past decade she has researched and written about the region's natural history.*

A Song for New-Ark

Nikki Giovanni

When I write I like to write . . . in total silence . . . Maybe total . . . silence . . . is not quite accurate . . . I like to listen to the notes breezing by my head . . . the grunting of the rainbow . . . as she bends . . . on her journey from Saturn . . . to harvest the melody . . .

There is no laughter . . . in the city . . . no joy . . . in the sheer delight . . . of living . . . City sounds . . . are the cracking of ice in glasses . . . or hearts in despair . . . The burglar alarms . . . or boredom . . . warning of illicit entry . . . The fire bells proclaiming . . . yet another home . . . or job . . . or dream . . . has deserted the will . . . to continue . . . The cries . . . of all the lonely people . . . for a drum . . . a tom-tom . . . some cymbal . . . some/body . . . to sing for . . .

I never saw old/jersey . . . or old/ark . . . Old/ark was a forest . . . felled for concrete . . . and asphalt . . . and bridges to Manhattan . . . Earth acres that once held families . . . of deer . . . fox . . . chipmunks . . . hawks . . . forest creatures . . . and their predators . . . now corral business . . . men and women . . . artists . . . and intellectuals . . . People . . . and their predators . . . under a banner of neon . . . graying the honest Black . . . cradling the stars above . . . and the earth below . . . turning to dust . . . white shirts . . . lace curtains at the

front window . . . automobiles lovingly polished . . . Dreams
. . . encountering racist resistance . . . New-Ark knows too
much pain . . . sees too many people who aren't special . . .
watches the buses daily . . . the churches on Sunday . . . the
bars after midnight . . . disgorge the unyoung . . . unable
. . . unqualified . . . unto the unaccepting . . . streets . . . I lived
. . . one summer . . . in New-Ark . . . New-Jersey . . . on Belleville
Avenue . . . Every evening . . . when the rats left the river . . . to
visit the central ward . . . Anthony Imperiali . . . and his boys
. . . would chunk bullets . . . at the fleeing mammals . . . refus-
ing to recognize . . . the obvious . . . family . . . ties . . . I napped
. . . to the rat-tat-tat . . . rat-tat-tat . . . wondering why . . . we
have yet to learn . . . rat-tat-tats . . . don't even impress . . .
rats . . .

When I write I want to write . . . in rhythm . . . regularizing
the moontides . . . to the heart/beats . . . of the twinkling
stars . . . sending an S.O.S. . . . to day trippers . . . urging them
to turn back . . . toward the Darkness . . . to ride the night
winds . . . to tomorrow . . . I wish I understood . . . bird . . .
Birds in the city talk . . . a city language . . . They always seem
. . . unlike humans . . . to have something . . . useful . . . to say
. . . Other birds . . . like Black americans . . . a century or so
ago . . . answer back . . . with song . . . I wish I could be a
melody . . . like a damp . . . gray . . . feline fog . . . staccatoing
. . . stealthily . . . over the city . . .

Nikki Giovanni *is the author of more than a dozen books of poetry
and a professor at Virginia Polytechnic Institute and State University.
Among many honors, she has been named woman of the year by*
Mademoiselle, Ladies Home Journal, *and* Ebony *magazines.*

Fledgling Summer

JENNIFER STANSBURY

with special thanks to Monica Hansen

~

People aren't the only ones who flock to Long Island's beaches in the summer. Many kinds of shorebirds gather on the beaches to lay their eggs and raise their young. In this essay, Jennifer Stansbury describes what it was like to spend a summer as a field biologist on Long Island studying roseate terns and other nesting birds.

~

Even as a young girl, watching nature shows and playing in the woods around my house, I knew I wanted to be a biologist. In 1987 I had just finished college, and I was to spend one summer on Long Island, in a beach community not far from New York City. But it wasn't for a family vacation or a typical summer job. I had been hired by Joanna Burger, a research scientist and professor at Rutgers University in New Jersey, to collect data on terns. I saw this job as my introduction to a career as a scientist. I was excited, especially to work with an endangered species, but I was also scared. I wasn't sure of myself or whether I could do a good job.

Terns are shorebirds in the same family as gulls, but they are smaller, with black caps on their heads and forked tails.

Known for their long seasonal migrations, these long-lived birds have straight sharp bills and pointed wings ideal for diving for fish in the ocean. They live in crowded colonies on the beaches and marshes of the barrier islands. The main focus of the study was to compare the endangered roseate terns to the common terns that dominated the colony.

Joanna was coordinating her studies with those of her former graduate student Carl Safina, who had hired half a dozen interns for the summer. The interns had their own jobs to do, but they also had to take turns helping me with my daily task of weighing and measuring chicks. We traveled each work day from the main island to work on land owned and protected by the Nature Conservancy.

We were housed in an old castlelike mansion. I was the only one with a room on the third floor, which I accessed by a dark, narrow, turning stairway. It was spooky at night to climb those stairs alone to an isolated room. Once there, I could look out one narrow window squeezed between the thick stone walls of the "castle."

The place was dank, very much like an actual castle. But with its large rooms, turrets, and French doors, it hinted of splendor. And though I longed to take strolls in the evening to explore the grounds, I could not. The wooded property, now a wildlife sanctuary, consisted of swampy wetlands that produced swarms of large mosquitoes.

Every evening the large kitchen was a lively, bustling place as each of us prepared our separate meals. We took turns at the stove and the shower, and at telling of our adventures in the field.

The Birds

I remember the first time I saw the colony on Cedar Beach. Carl and Joanna drove me up from New Jersey, past the huge garbage dumps on Staten Island and over the long bridges that led to Long Island and the barrier island. The colony included hundreds of nesting pairs of common terns along with roseate terns, black skimmers, and other birds. Their nesting areas were surrounded by a fence that separated them from the adjacent public beach. It was spring, before the hordes of summer visitors came to escape their unair-conditioned houses. And it was before the flocks of birds, migrating north from the tropics, reached their most numerous. It seemed very peaceful and beautiful. Peaceful, that is, until we squeezed through a break in the fence into the birds' nesting area. The birds took to the air and mobbed us with screeching voices.

Once our summer field season began, we quickly became accustomed to the endless bombardment of hard pecks on our helmets and the constant high-pitched rasping of the birds defending their nests and young. Agile flyers, the terns would sometimes pull at the hair poking out from under my helmet at the nape of my neck. They even used their fecal matter as a weapon. We would go home covered with bird poop—a variety of colors and consistencies, depending on the types of fish the terns were eating. We'd get tan lines on our arms and legs in the shape of splatters. Even our data sheets were not spared. The birds had very good aim. Once I got hit with poop on the inside of my sunglasses but got nothing in my eye. It was especially tough when I was assigned to count the number of individuals mobbing at a particular time and location. Normally when we were weighing and measuring chicks in the nest, we would keep our heads down, tolerate the assault, and shout to the person right by us to be heard over the roar. But when I had to count the birds in the air, I had to expose my face to the onslaught. I could see them jockey for position, screaming when they'd get too close to each other or touch wings. Then they would take turns swooping down with a screech at me and a hit. The birds' impeccable aim would remind me to count with my mouth closed.

The birds were not trying to protect the entire colony, only their own young. So once we left the vicinity of their own nests, they would settle down. As we moved to the next section of the colony, we would rouse another group, inviting them to return the harassment we inflicted on them. I had thought birds were not intelligent creatures. Then Carl told us that the terns learned to recognize his vehicle and would begin mobbing him in the parking lot, before he even reached the colony. Interestingly, though, they would leave Joanna alone; she didn't even bother to wear a helmet. They must not have felt as threatened by her because she often came to sit and watch rather than disturb their nests as we were instructed to do daily.

I'd often wish I had time to sit and watch. I would have watched the terns' behavior—how they interacted with their neighbors, how they treated their young. I would have watched their sleek, streamlined bodies navigate the wind, the way they walked awkwardly on short legs with flat feet, and many other things. But there was no time for me to sit and watch. I had to check about a hundred roseate tern nests and fifty common tern nests each day I was in the field. And in my spare time, I had to estimate the percentage cover of plants near each nest on my list (and at random points too), estimate the number of mobbing adults, search for undiscovered roseate tern nests, and record the weather conditions. All this was important in order to learn as much as possible. Without information, there is no way to help an endangered species. But whenever I could, I'd search out a roseate adult circling around the perimeter of the mob of common terns. Less aggressive and more beautiful, with longer tails and blacker beaks, the roseates were stunning against the blue sky. When I'd spot one, the noise of the mob would go quiet in my head. This was why *I* was here.

Nesting

The terns' nests were scattered all over the beach—a varied habitat of flat, open ground between mounds and small dunes covered with beach grasses, broadleaf plants, and small shrubs. The nests consisted merely of shallow scrapes in the sand with the eggs sitting there in the open. Some of the depressions contained a few twigs, grass, or shells—almost as a token effort toward a true nest. Early in the season, a few nests got stepped on, crushing the eggs. It happened as easily as someone stepping backward to shift his weight. We quickly learned to watch our *every* step. I felt so awful, like we were huge clumsy intruders—and we were. I questioned our presence in the colony.

As part of our work, we had to learn to distinguish between the nests of the two species. Roseate terns usually sited their nests close to plants. These locations may have provided more protection from the heat or from aerial predators. Although the eggs of both roseates and common terns were speckled and blotchy, they differed slightly in color and shape. Also, the roseates usually laid one or two eggs per clutch, while many of the common terns laid three. Once the chicks hatched, it was much easier to tell them apart. Roseate chicks were gray, and their feathers were not as fluffy as those of the tawny yellow common tern chicks.

Monitoring the nests daily, I got to know each one, and I waited eagerly for the milestone of hatching as one waits for the first word or first step of a child. The same kind of excitement and happiness filled me when I witnessed a crack in a shell or a newly hatched chick, panting as it dried into a little fuzz ball. Likewise, I was saddened when some of the eggs never hatched. Also, I became fond of certain nests—the unusual three-egg clutch of a roseate, or a nest I myself had discovered. Every day I checked my nests for their progress and condition. The eggs were laid one or two days apart, so the chicks hatched one or two days apart. Thus the oldest chick of a clutch was always larger than its siblings.

As soon as a chick was born, we would band it. To do this well, without squeezing the leg or crimping the metal band, took practice. We had to make sure the band was smooth and could move up and down on the leg without injury. After the chicks were hatched, we would measure their weight and the lengths of their beaks, wing tips, and tarsus (the part where the band is placed, which is actually part of the foot), and record the time of day. We had to complete our task at each nest as quickly as possible so the attending adult could return to the young. The eggs and chicks needed shelter from the hot sun or the rain. Of course the adults, with their noise and dive-bombing, made sure we didn't forget to make haste, their confidence increasing as the summer wore on.

We banded some of the adults, too, but unlike the chicks, they had to be trapped first. With Carl's supervision, we placed traps that were like metal wire cages over three or four nests at a time, careful not to crush the eggs. Most of the adults would walk right into the trap as though it weren't there. We watched, and as soon as all the traps were sprung, we hurried to collect them. One at a time, we took the birds out, performed the usual measurements, banded, and released them. It was extra special for me to handle the adults, to see them up close and feel their soft feathers. But again, skill and care were in order. The birds were held gently but firmly by their legs and waist, with their wings tucked in. Carl told us to be careful not to squeeze their chests because their air passages, so crucial to flight, could easily be damaged.

We would always break for lunch by the ocean waves. I had a peanut butter and jelly sandwich every day because I liked nothing else, a juice box, and chips. It was such a relief after working all morning in the heavy heat and bright sand to actually see the ocean, cool off in the waves, and just sit for a spell. We enjoyed talking and watching the piping plover chicks follow their mother and forage for food along the water's edge. The tiny, very endangered birds had legs that moved in a blur beneath them, and they made the sweetest monotone sound, like a flute. It was always hard to pick up and head back to work.

Threats

The privilege of handling wild birds endeared them to me, but that only made things harder once nature showed me her cruelty. Sometimes a chick would begin its tiring task of cracking its eggshell, pecking to break free, then resting, and pecking again. Only it would never get out. Ants would discover the egg, its shell no longer intact. They would crawl through the hole in the shell and kill the chick—before it could see the sunlight or taste a fish, and long before it could meet the promise of flight. Sometimes a chick would suffer an ant attack after hatching, being painfully bitten all over by an unknown force, aware of nothing but its suffering.

The terns themselves were no more sympathetic. Nesting together in a colony afforded them some safety from predators, but their close proximity did not make them friendly neighbors. Things weren't too bad until the chicks were old enough to wander from their own scrapes in the sand. Parents chased away any chicks that were not their own. This behavior is expected in a colonial situation, but I was not prepared for the brutality of it. One day I noticed a chick, strangely alone. As I approached, I could see a bright red bead of blood on its head. It took me a moment to comprehend that the injury was caused by a neighboring adult. At that moment, my romantic notions of nature were gone.

On that day I became very grateful I didn't have to struggle and fight for my very life. Grateful I didn't have to worry about predators like the terns did—mammals by night, gulls by day. I remember being by the water at the end of the day, walking toward the beach house, and seeing a gull flying with a tern chick in its beak. It dropped it on the hard sand. Right then I hated the gulls. But I could not blame the scavengers for utilizing a helpless and plentiful food resource.

The terns also battled the weather. During a big storm midseason we humans retreated to the safety and comfort of the mansion, but the birds had to stick it out on the beach. Some didn't make it. Upon our return to the field, the beach was changed. Debris and sand had been shifted around. Some nests had been completely washed away.

Then, late in the season, when the chicks were nearing fledgling age, sickness swept across the colony. Victims were seen walking in circles, unable to control their movements, before they died. It became more clear why adults would be so determined to protect their own chicks from possibly infected neighbors.

Humans, too, posed a threat to the birds. Although the colony was fenced off, we occasionally had to chase people out of the nesting area anyway. They crossed it as a shortcut to the beach, unaware that they could easily tread on the eggs of endangered species. I'll admit that at times I was a bit envious of the beachgoers. They were there to play and relax. They could get in the water to cool off when I had to march the shadeless sand with poop all over me. But their bliss was in ignorance, and it was ignorance that was endangering these birds. The trash they carelessly left behind was hazardous to the birds and the other creatures that inhabit the ocean and shoreline.

The worst of it by far was the fishing line. I was exposed to the evils of the endless, unbreakable, invisible, indigestible stuff when a fishing line was found one day on the beach. It was stretched across the colony for about one third, or perhaps even half, of the nesting area's length. We gathered it up, untangling birds as we went. Only some were still alive. I remember one victim vividly: fishing line wrapped many times around its tarsus, cutting through bloody skin. We freed it, but we couldn't know if it would survive.

Summer's End

At the end of the season, the colony looked very different. Early on, there were eggs or chicks in the nests and adults flying above, but now there were birds running all over the ground, exercising and stretching their wings, trying to fly. The chicks were getting ready to join their parents on the migration. The interns and I were sent out with strings of bands. We were systematically to band as many birds as we could of the hundreds not included in the nest monitoring. No longer concerned with stepping on eggs, we ran, chasing juveniles who would often out maneuver us. Sometimes they would surprise us, and themselves, when, after trying to outrun us, they would take off into the air, and out of our reach. We'd have to give up that chase for another. Once we caught a runner, we would band it and gently toss it into the air. If it couldn't fly it would flap down to the ground, but once in a while, it would fly. It would fledge, right out of our hands. Imagine the feeling and the surprise of the first flight!

And then the field season was finished. I was glad to be done with the heat, the biting flies, and the stench of my clothes and data papers. Taking a final visit to the beach, I looked at the transformed colony, which I now saw as both nursery and battleground. I would miss the ocean, watching the terns in flight, and seeing the eggs nestled together in the sand. I would miss the killdeer calling me away from her nest, pretending she had a broken wing, only to fly and try again in a different spot. I would miss the tiny piping plovers, funny little puffballs on stilts, and the black skimmers standing together, still as statues.

It was also time to leave my summer sanctuary, the "castle" in the woods. I took my final drive out the winding gravel road. It was lined with towering rhododendrons, which when I had arrived were in full bloom. Now they were plain green. Science, I had learned, was not glamorous, or even glorious. It was tedious, disruptive, and unsure. But understanding nature was empowering. I had been privileged to walk the colony, and had proudly worn those splattered clothes.

~⌐

Jennifer Stansbury *is a biologist who now enjoys watching the behavior and development of her two young children at her home in Laramie, Wyoming.*

Golden-Crowned Kinglet

Tyler Cadman

This afternoon
as I sat in the woods,
the sun piercing the canopy,

I saw in the corner
of my eye a small bird
fluttering from branch to branch.

Chirping in its high voice
it drifted toward me,
vibrating the branches

as it landed,
touching down on the
branch next to me.

It cocked its head.
Its golden crest flashed in
the bright light.

For a magical moment it
looked me in the eye.
When it flew away

I wondered why
I do not make the time
for more moments

like
this
one.

Tyler Cadman *lives in Westport Island, Maine, and is a student at the Center for Teaching and Learning. He wrote "Golden-Crowned Kinglet" when he was twelve years old.*

Never Go Home
without a Fish

GRETCHEN WOELFLE

This tale is based on an event that took place on Damariscotta Lake around 1850, but we suspect that even today one can find fishermen on the lakes of Maine exhibiting the same kind of stubborn persistence.

"Let's go fishing tomorrow," Christopher said to Uncle Johnathan.

"We'll pack our food tonight and leave before dawn," his uncle replied.

Uncle Johnathan never went home without a fish, so he carried enough food to last the whole day: bread, butter, and salt pork for breakfast; more of the same with cheese and apple pie for lunch; and doughnuts for snacks in between. "I don't weigh 260 pounds by eating light," Uncle Johnathan allowed.

At the shore Christopher cut saplings for fishing poles. "Thick as my index finger on one end, thin as a pencil on the tip," said Uncle Johnathan. They tied on twenty feet of linen line, then tied hooks on the end of the line.

Christopher rowed to their favorite cove. He filled a bucket with water and lowered a sieve into the lake. He threw bread crumbs on the surface, and soon a school of minnows swarmed to eat the crumbs. Christopher raised the sieve and dropped the minnows into the bucket.

"Good start," said Uncle Johnathan.

The sun rose as they baited their hooks, cast their lines, and watched a kingfisher dive for its breakfast.

Morning came and went.

No fish.

"Nothing's happening," complained Christopher.

"Fishing is mostly waiting," said his uncle as they rowed ashore for lunch.

Uncle Johnathan poked through the lunch bucket. "I'm tired of salt pork," he said. "Fried fish will taste mighty good for supper."

Uncle Johnathan got ready for a nap. He stuck his pole in the sand with a mess of sticks and string and a spare fish hook that would lift his hat if he got a bite.

"Never let the fish know you're sleeping," he said.

Christopher stuck his pole in the sand too, but he needed his hat for picking blueberries. He filled it nearly full, but the tiny berries tasted so good he ate half a hatful before Uncle Johnathan woke up.

"Save some for later," his uncle said. "We won't go home without a fish."

During the afternoon they anchored near a rock ledge and floated in the weeds. They rowed toward the narrows and fished with worms as well as minnows.

"I hate all this waiting," Christopher said. "I'm going for a swim." He swam round the boat. He dove underneath and thumped the bottom to give Uncle Johnathan a start. Finally he climbed back in.

"Good night for fishing," said his uncle looking to the sky.

"We can wait all night for a fish, right, Uncle Johnathan?" He tried to keep the excitement out of his voice.

They ate leftover lunch for supper and watched the sun set behind the hills. A breeze made orange and pink ripples on the water, and a great blue heron glided by.

"Hoo ooo ooo ooo," called a loon. "Hoo ooo ooo ooo," came an answer across the lake. Stars came out. Christopher picked out constellations—the Big Bear, the Little Bear, Leo the Lion.

"Tell me about the ice-skating contest," Christopher said. It was his favorite story, and it happened right here on the lake.

"All the other skaters were young and lean. I was middle-aged and fat." His uncle chuckled. "They dragged logs out onto the ice and took turns jumping. One log, then two, four, eight, twelve logs. They laughed every time I took my turn, but I laughed back."

Christopher could picture Uncle Johnathan heaving his big body from side to side, swinging his arms back and forth.

"At sixteen logs, only three skaters were left, and one was me. At nineteen logs, another man fell. Then there was just young Bill Bixby and me. We both jumped twenty logs. Then at twenty-one, Billy nicked his skate on the last log and skidded for fifty feet. You should have heard him howl. I cleared it. Then for good measure, I jumped over another one. Twenty-two logs. No one has ever beaten my record." He chuckled again.

"Life gives you things you never expect," Uncle Johnathan mused, "and sometimes it doesn't give you what you have every right to expect—like a fish for dinner!" He paused, then continued, "Hornpouts come out at night. They'll taste good for breakfast."

Uncle Johnathan kept fishing. Christopher lay down with his jacket under his head. The rocking boat lulled him to sleep. He awoke to hear Uncle Johnathan singing.

I'm lonesome since I crossed the hill,
And o'er the moor and valley;
Such heavy thoughts my heart do fill,
Since parting with my Sally.

I seek no more the fine and gay,
For each does but remind me
How swift the hours did pass away
With the girl I left behind me.

That was something Christopher didn't expect. He'd never heard his uncle sing before. The boy felt he was floating . . . above the boat . . . above the earth. . . . When he woke again, Uncle Johnathan was asleep, his fishing pole in his hand.

The moonlight wiggled on the lake like a giant silver snake. He swished his hand through the water. It felt warm. A bat whooshed past, and a solitary fish splashed across the lake. He remembered his uncle's lonesome song. Had Uncle Johnathan ever had a sweetheart?

Christopher lay down again. Mist swirled around the boat when he woke, but he saw a rosy glow in the east. Uncle Johnathan was still sleeping, his head on his chest.

The moon grew dim as the sky brightened. Finally the sun burst over the pine trees and blazed on the water, scattering the mist. Christopher jumped into the lake and came up hollering. The cold water chased the sleepiness from his body.

Uncle Johnathan woke with a start and dropped his fishing pole overboard. Christopher laughed so hard he swallowed water and started sputtering.

"When you're done laughing, would you mind fetching my pole?" his uncle asked. "It's floating away."

With a few strong strokes, Christopher caught the pole, then lay on his back and kicked back to the boat. "Never let a fish catch you sleeping, Uncle Johnathan."

"Humph," grunted his uncle, but the corners of his mouth turned up.

Christopher saw two soggy doughnuts and some blueberries in the bucket. "Blueberries or doughnuts?" Christopher asked.

"Save the best for last. We won't go home without a fish," his uncle said as he reached for a doughnut.

When would that be? thought Christopher. Would they stay out for days and nights until they caught a fish? At noon they ate the blueberries. Christopher's feet fell asleep. He rubbed them against the boat.

"Have you ever fished this long before?" asked Christopher.

"Nope." Uncle Johnathan pressed his lips together.

"Well," said the boy, "life gives us things we never expect."

Christopher was daydreaming about creamy fish chowder when he felt a tug on his line. A yellow perch thrashed about underwater, its golden flanks glittering in the sunlight.

"Easy there," his uncle said. Christopher pulled the line out, then brought it closer. The perch swam to the rocks. If the line snagged, the fish might get away.

Uncle Johnathan rowed so Christopher could pull the fish straight out of the water. His uncle caught the perch in the net, and Christopher dropped it in the pail.

"Well done," said Uncle Johnathan.

An arrow of orange afternoon light shot across the lake.

"Can we go home," Christopher asked, "if I give you my fish?"

Uncle Johnathan stared at his nephew. Christopher knew the answer: Uncle Johnathan had to catch his own fish.

A few minutes later Christopher cried, "I've got it! Uncle Johnathan, is there any salt pork left?"

"I'm not hungry."

"Is there?"

"Just a hunk of rind."

"Well then, we'll give the fish something *they* don't expect." Christopher took out his pocket knife. "I'll carve a frog with the pork rind!"

"By golly, why didn't I think of that?" exclaimed Uncle Johnathan.

"Because we've been saving the best till last," said the boy.

When Christopher had carved his frog, he scraped away the fat from under the legs. Then he shook it. The frog body was firm, but the legs wiggled. It might fool a fish.

Christopher attached the frog to the hook, and Uncle Johnathan pulled it to and fro on the water. It skittered among the lily pads.

Suddenly a fish grabbed for it. Uncle Johnathan pulled his line, but the fish got away.

"I'll row in a circle," Christopher said. "We know he's in there."

Back and forth Uncle Johnathan guided his frog. The lily pads trembled.

Splash! The fish bit the frog's leg, then vanished.

"Third time lucky," muttered Uncle Johnathan, pulling the frog a little quicker.

Snap! The fish grabbed the whole frog in its mouth. Uncle Johnathan eased him closer, then out of the water. It was a smallmouth bass, his favorite.

"Hooray for Uncle Johnathan!" shouted Christopher, stamping his feet.

His uncle looked at the two fish in the bucket. "Well, we've got our fish . . ."

Christopher chimed in, ". . . so we can go home!"

Gretchen Woelfle *writes children's stories and environmental nonfiction in Venice, California. Johnathan Ames, a distant relative of hers, really did weigh 260 pounds, did jump over twenty-two logs on ice skates, and did stay out for thirty-six hours until he caught a fish on Damariscotta Lake in Maine.*

The Beech Tree

W. D. Ehrhart

My neighbor leans across the fence
and gestures upward grandly, making
with his two arms a tiny human
imitation of a beech tree lifting
two hundred years of sprawling growth.
"Quite a tree you've got!" he says.
"By God, I wish I owned it."

But though it lives in my backyard,
this tree belongs to the squirrels
leaping branches just beyond my window.
"You'd like to catch us, but you can't,"
they seem to scold the tabby cat
that crouches daily with a patience
too dim to comprehend the squirrels
own this tree and will not fall.

It belongs to the robins that nested
last year in a high sheltered fork.

It belongs to the insects burrowing
beneath its aging bark like miners.

I'm just the janitor: raking leaves,
pruning limbs to keep them from collapsing
the garage roof next door or climbing
into bed beside my wife and me.

Possession is a curious thing:
some things are not for owning,
and I don't mind caring for a tree
that isn't mine. I take my pay
in April reawakening and summer shade.
Just now, I'm watching snow
collecting in the upper branches,
waiting for the robins to come home.

W. D. Ehrhart *is the author or editor of seventeen books of prose and poetry, most recently* Beautiful Wreckage: New and Selected Poems *from Adastra Press. He wrote "The Beech Tree" while waiting not only for the robins to come home but also for the arrival of his daughter Leela, who was born just days after the poem was written.*

Wild Lives

Glooskap and the Whale

JOSEPH BRUCHAC

This story comes from the Micmac, native peoples of Newfoundland and the Canadian Maritimes. According to Micmac legend, Glooskap was a giant, a trickster, and a creator. He was said to have slept across Nova Scotia, using Prince Edward Island for his pillow.

Long ago, Glooskap lived on an island. He came down to the shore, wanting to cross over to the mainland. He had no boat and the water was deep. So he began to sing a song:

> Podawawogan,
> Whale come and help me,
> Podawawogan,
> Help me to cross

His song had great power and soon a whale rose to the surface of the water and swam close in the deep water to the place where Glooskap stood. This whale, though, was not a big whale and Glooskap was a giant. Glooskap put one foot on the whale's back. As soon as he began to put his weight onto the whale it sank. Glooskap pulled his foot back.

"Thank you, brother," he said, "but you are not strong enough to carry me."

Then Glooskap sang his song again:

Podawawogan,
Whale come and help me,
Podawawogan,
Help me to cross

This time, the largest of all the whales came. It was a huge female, her blue back so wide that Glooskap could easily climb on board. Soon she was swimming through the waves, heading for the mainland.

This great whale, though, was worried about going aground. She knew that the water grew shallow close to the mainland. Glooskap, however, did not want to get his feet wet. Before long, they started to get close to shore.

"Can you see the land from my back?" the great whale said.

The land was now in sight, but Glooskap was afraid she would dive and leave him in the water if he told the truth.

"No," he said, "land is still out of sight. Swim faster, Grandmother, swim faster."

Then the whale began to swim faster. But as she swam, she looked down and she could see the shells of the clams below her. This frightened her, for she knew that meant the water was no longer so deep.

"Can you see the land from my back," she said, "doesn't it show itself like the string of a bow?"

"No," Glooskap said, "we're still far from land. Swim faster, Grandmother, swim faster."

Now the clams did not like Glooskap. He had gathered many of them and eaten them, making great mounds of empty shells on the shore. The clams began to sing:

You are close to land,
throw him off, thrown him off,
You are close to land,
throw him off, let him drown

"What are the clams singing?" the great whale said. She could not understand their language.

"Ah," Glooskap said, "I can understand them. They are saying to hurry, to hurry along. To hurry along for we're still far from shore."

"Then I must hurry," the whale said. She dove with her mighty tail—and found herself grounded up on the beach! She was stuck and could not get free.

Glooskap climbed from her back.

"Grandchild," the great whale said, "you have been my death. I will never swim in the sea again."

Glooskap shook his head. "No, Grandmother," he said. "I will not let you suffer. You will swim in the sea again." He pulled his great bow from his back and pushed with it against the great whale's head. He pushed her from the beach and back into the deep water again.

The whale was very happy. She leaped and danced in the waves, throwing great mountains of spray up as she breached. To this day the great whales dance that way, remembering how Glooskap pushed their grandmother back into the water. Then the whale turned back towards Glooskap.

"Grandchild," she said, "can you give me something?"

Glooskap took his pipe from his pouch. "I will give you this, Grandmother," he said.

The great whale took the pipe. To this day you may see the big whales blowing the smoke up into the air from that pipe which Glooskap gave their grandmother when she helped him come to the mainland.

Joseph Bruchac *has authored more than fifty books for adults and children. Of part Abenaki descent, he is a scholar of Native American culture and was honored in 1999 with the Lifetime Achievement Award of the Native Writers' Circle.*

Starfish

MARY OLIVER

In the sea rocks,
    in the stone pockets
        under the tide's lip,
            in water dense as blindness

they slid
    like sponges,
        like too many thumbs.
            I knew this, and what I wanted

was to draw my hands back
    from the water—what I wanted
        was to be willing
            to be afraid.

But I stayed there,
    I crouched on the stone wall
        while the sea poured its harsh song
            through the sluices,

while I waited for the gritty lightning
    of their touch, while I stared

down through the tide's leaving
where sometimes I could see them—

their stubborn flesh
lounging on my knuckles.
What good does it do
to lie all day in the sun

loving what is easy?
It never grew easy,
but at last I grew peaceful:
all summer

my fear diminished
as they bloomed through the water
like flowers, like flecks
of an uncertain dream,

while I lay on the rocks, reaching
into the darkness, learning
little by little to love
our only world.

Mary Oliver *is a Pulitzer Prize-winning poet and the author of more than seven poetry collections. She was born in Cleveland, Ohio, and has lived in Provincetown, Massachusetts, since 1964. She currently teaches at Bennington College.*

Otter Delight

DAVID SOBEL

River otters are energetic and playful, known for cavorting in the water and sliding headlong down stream banks. What would it be like to spend a day following in an otter's tracks? David Sobel tells us in this essay.

The tracks left the stream below the beaver pond and just above the waterfall. Perhaps the otter was avoiding my house, located near the base of the falls. More likely, she was taking a timeworn shortcut. Quick bounds up the bank were recorded in her tracks. Then, on level ground, her stride became syncopated: run, run, slide . . . run, run, slide. Her slides formed a carved trough of pliant snow; even going slightly uphill, she continued this rhythm. Across the lichened stone wall and then downhill, she executed a single glissade, sinuously slithering around trees, like water flowing along the path of least resistance. At the beaver pond below my house she rejoined the stream, moving onward.

Like brooks, otters move with effortless strength. They are always traveling, often covering ten miles in a day. Yet they take time to dawdle in eddies, careen down banks, and do corkscrew turns and double one-and-a-half gainers in pursuit of fish. I envy both their energy and their diversity of movement. While skiing, I try to imitate the thrust of otters in snow, streamlining forward, their legs clamped to their sides. If I could achieve the same purposeful thrust and remain spontaneously sensitive to the topography underfoot, my skiing would be perfect.

The otter that had jaunted past my house was probably traveling part of a winter circuit. In southern New Hampshire, where most bodies of water freeze hard from December to March, otters often need to range far afield to visit a variety of feeding spots. They search out warm springs, fast-water rapids, or active beaver ponds that allow them access to the under-ice world. This otter probably came across the divide from the Great White Swamp into Bailey Brook, past my house to Robb Marsh, then along the swampy reaches of the North Branch, into the Contoocook drainage, and up the Nubanusit to Spoonwood and the swamp. Or she might be traveling the North Branch and its numerous swampy setbacks. Her circuit might be up to forty miles around, taking up to two weeks to complete. And since otter populations average only one per six to ten square miles, this is probably the same individual that passed my house a month ago.

I set off a few days later to track the otter. The mid-February rains followed by a freeze had produced a hard and glassy ice. I skated the meandering marshy streams, through the muskrat and beaver swamps, following the frozen slush trail of the otter. The post-rain soggy snow had not slowed her progress. I could see sprays of slush from her sliding, frozen near her tracks. Underneath the sultry black ice, air bubbles were trapped eight inches beneath my feet. Using these bubbles, otters can stretch their under-ice time from the regular two-to-four minutes to an hour.

Approaching the rapids below Robb Marsh, I slowed down.

Piles of scaly and chitinous scat were evident near the ice's edge, but no otter. Evidently, she was eating perch, pickerel, and crayfish. Contrary to prevalent myths, otters do not solely eat game fish. In fact, an all-fish diet can kill an otter (piscivores, take note). Otters eat crayfish when it is available and a wide variety of forage fish as well as game fish. Being unselective, they also regularly dine on frogs, salamanders, and aquatic insects; they certainly are undeserving of their reputation as trout murderers. But because of the lack of variety in wintry food, this otter was taking primarily fish.

I skated with long, cutting strokes to the rapids two miles

distant and in time heard the noise of quick water ahead. I approached and peered around a willow thicket: there she was. She tossed her head back and chewed, fish bones grinding. Another bite and her head arched again, sniffing the air. She slipped into the icy water, and I could imagine her quick undulations propelling her forward toward a pickerel, the fish dashing for cover amid the bank sedges, red-maple roots, and mazes of beaver-felled poplars, the otter catching the faint glint of the pickerel's scales, hovering, darting, twisting, and grabbing it behind the head. She came back up on the ice in a liquid swoop, her whiskers twitching as she chomped down the Y-bones. I thought her food would preoccupy her enough to make her unaware of my presence, and I inched forward. She glanced in my direction and was underwater in an instant. She thrust her head through the surface as if standing on a rock and examined me for a moment, then dove and was gone.

I waited, but she had retired to a hideout beneath the ice, either to the abandoned beaver lodge nearby or the hollow created by a felled tree beneath the snow and ice. Otters thrive in these vegetative labyrinths. I remember creeping through such tunnels when I was young, and I tried to imagine swimming through them now in the gray-green gloom. She was down there, cleaning her fur, snuggling into the warm grass and mud.

I skated on to Ball Basin, an assemblage of swamps, marshes, and wide expanses of ice. Numerous stream basins opened like rooms onto the central sweep of ice. No otter was to be found, but at the upper reach of each marshy expanse there was an unusual playground. Each stream had frozen into a gentle-tiered ice floe, the rain and cold synthesized into a melted wedding cake. I herringboned my way to the top, lay down on my stomach, and streamlined my hands to my sides. Slithering down the ice floe, I pushed off from a frozen rock with my hip, following the icy contours of the stream and sharing the otter's sinuous grace for a moment.

David Sobel *directs the elementary teacher certification program at Antioch New England Graduate School. He is the author of several nonfiction books about children and the natural world, including* Children's Special Places, Beyond Ecophobia: Reclaiming the Heart in Nature Education, *and* Mapmaking with Children: Sense of Place Education for the Elementary Years.

Long Island Crow

NORBERT KRAPF

He soars darkly above cars
crawling bumper to bumper

toward Manhattan, glides in a circle
above treetops in the village park,

climbs above apartment complexes
toward a grove of oaks

on the highest ridge in the county.
He perches, gazes back down

at the valley, and caws forth
from the shadows of his brain

a thick forest in which morning
campfire smoke rises like mist.

Norbert Krapf *grew up in southern Indiana but has lived on Long Island since 1970. The director of the C. W. Post Poetry Center of Long Island University, he is the author of several books, including* Somewhere in Southern Indiana, Blue-Eyed Grass: Poems of Germany, *and the forthcoming* Bittersweet Along the Expressway. *He has a special interest in the relationship between literature and place.*

The Great Whale

FARLEY MOWAT

In the winter of 1967, a seventy-foot whale became trapped in a pond in Burgeo, Newfoundland. The pond was connected to the Atlantic by a narrow channel that became deep enough for the whale to swim through during an unusually high tide. In the following excerpt, author and naturalist Farley Mowat responds to news of the whale's existence and to the rumor that local islanders have been taking shots at her for sport.

Early next morning I telephoned Danny Green, a lean, sardonic and highly intelligent man in his middle thirties who had been the high-lining skipper of a dragger but had given that up to become skipper, mate and crew of the little Royal Canadian Mounted Police motor launch. Danny not only knew—and was happy to comment on—everything of importance that happened on the Sou'west Coast, he was also familiar with and interested in whales. What he had to tell me brought my excitement to fever pitch.

"I'm pretty sure 'tis one of the big ones, Farley. Can't say what kind. Haven't seen it meself but it might be a Humpback, a Finner or even a Sulphur." He paused a moment. "What's left of it. The sports have been blasting hell out of it this past week."

As Danny gave me further details of what had been happening, I was at first appalled, then furious.

"Are they bloody well crazy? This is a chance in a million. If that whale lives, Burgeo'll be famous all over the world. *Shooting* at it! What the hell's the matter with the constable?"

Danny explained that our one policeman was a temporary replacement for the regular constable, who was away on leave. The new man, Constable Murdoch, was from New Brunswick. He knew nothing about Burgeo and not much about Newfoundland. He was hesitant to interfere in local matters unless he received an official complaint.

At my request, Danny put him on the phone.

"Whoever's doing that shooting is breaking the game laws, you know," I told him. "It's forbidden to take rifles into the country. Can't you put a stop to it?"

Murdoch was apologetic and cooperative. Not only did he undertake to investigate the shooting, he offered to make a patrol to Aldridges Pond and take me with him. However, Claire and I had already made other arrangements with two Messers fishermen, Curt Bungay and Wash Pink, who fished together in Curt's new boat. They were an oddly assorted pair. Young, and newly married, Curt was one of those people about whom the single adjective, "round," says it all. His crimson-hued face was a perfect circle, with round blue eyes, a round little nose, and a circular mouth. Although he was not fat, his body was a cylinder supported on legs as round and heavy as mill logs. Wash Pink was almost the complete opposite. A much older man, who had known hard times in a distant outport, he was lean, desiccated, and angular. And whereas Curt was a born talker and storyteller, Wash seldom opened his mouth except in moments of singular stress.

A few minutes after talking to Murdoch, Claire and I were under way in Curt's longliner. I was dithering between hope that we would find a great whale in the Pond, alive and well, and the possibility that it might have escaped or, even worse, have succumbed to the shooting. Claire kept her usual cool head, as her notes testify:

"It was blowing about 40 miles an hour from the north-west," she wrote, "and I hesitated to go along. But Farley said I would regret it all my life if I didn't. Burgeo being Burgeo, it wouldn't have surprised me if the 'giant whale' had turned out to be a porpoise. It was rough and icy cold crossing Short Reach but we got to Aldridges all right and sidled cautiously through the narrow channel. It was several hours from high tide and there was only five feet of water, which made Curt very nervous for the safety of his brand-new boat.

"We slid into the pretty little Pond under a dash of watery sunlight. It was a beautifully protected natural harbour ringed with rocky cliffs that ran up to the 300-foot crest of Richards Head. Little clumps of dwarfed black spruce clung in the hollows here and there along the shore.

"There was nobody and nothing to be seen except a few gulls soaring high overhead. We looked eagerly for signs of the whale, half expecting it to come charging out of nowhere and send us scurrying for the exit. There was no sign of it and I personally concluded it had left— if it had ever been in the Pond at all.

"I was ready to go below and try to get warm when somebody cried out that they saw something. We all looked and saw a long, black shape that looked like a giant sea-serpent, curving quietly out of the water, and slipping along from head to fin, and then down again and out of sight.

"We just stared, speechless and unbelieving, at this vast monster. Then there was a frenzy of talk.

"'It's a *whale* of a whale! . . . Must be fifty, sixty feet long! . . . That's no Pothead, not that one . . .'

"Indeed, it was no Pothead but an utterly immense, solitary and lonely monster, trapped, Heaven knew how, in this rocky prison.

"We chugged to the middle of the Pond just as the R.C.M.P launch entered and headed for us. Farley called to Danny Green and they agreed to anchor the two boats in deep water near the south end of the Pond and stop the engines.

"Then began a long, long watch during which the hours went by like minutes. It was endlessly fascinating to watch the almost serpentine coming and going of this huge beast. It would surface about every four or five minutes as it followed a circular path around and around the Pond. At first the circles took it well away from us but as time passed, and everyone kept perfectly still, the circles narrowed, coming closer and closer to the boats.

"Twice the immense head came lunging out of the water high into the air. It was as big as a small house, glistening black on top and fish-white underneath. Then down would go the nose, and the blowhole would break surface, and then the long, broad back, looking like the bottom of an overturned ship, would slip into our sight. Finally the fin would appear, at least four feet tall, and then a boiling up of water from the flukes and the whale was gone again.

"Farley identified it as a Fin Whale, the second largest

animal ever to live on earth. We could see the marks of bullets—holes and slashes—across the back from the blowhole to
the fin. It was just beyond me to even begin to understand the
mentality of men who would amuse themselves filling such a
majestic creature full of bullets. Why *try* to kill it? There is no
mink or fox farm here to use the meat. None of the people
would eat it. No, there is no motive of food or profit; only a
lust to kill. But then I wonder, is it any different than the
killer's lust that makes the mainland sportsmen go out in
their big cars to slaughter rabbits or ground-hogs? It just
seems so much more terrible to kill a whale!

"We could trace its progress even under water by the
smooth, swirling tide its flukes left behind. It appeared to be
swimming only about six feet deep and it kept getting closer to
us so we began to catch glimpses of it under the surface, its
white underparts appearing pale aqua-green against the
darker background of deep water.

"The undulations on the surface came closer and closer
until the whale was surfacing within twenty feet of the boats.
It seemed to deliberately look at us from time to time as if trying to decide whether we were dangerous. Oddly, the thought
never crossed my mind that *it* might be dangerous to us. Later
on I asked some of the others if they had been afraid of this,
the mightiest animal any of us was ever likely to meet in all our
lives, and nobody had felt any fear at all. We were too en-
thralled to be afraid.

"Apparently the whale decided we were not dangerous. It
made another sweep and this time that mighty head passed
right under the Mountie's boat. They pointed and waved and
we stared down too. Along came the head, like a submarine,
but much more beautiful, slipping along under us no more

than six feet away. Just then Danny shouted: 'Here's his tail! Here's his tail!'

"The tail was just passing under the police launch while the head was under *our* boat, and the two boats were a good seventy feet apart! The flippers, each as long as a dory, showed green beneath us, then the whole unbelievable length of the body flowed under the boat, silently, with just a faint slick swirl of water on the surface from the flukes. It was almost impossible to believe what we were seeing! This incredibly vast being, perhaps eighty tons in weight, so Farley guessed, swimming below us with the ease and smoothness of a salmon.

"Danny told me later the whale could have smashed up both our boats as easily as we would smash a couple of eggs. Considering what people had done to it, why didn't it take revenge? Or is it only mankind that takes revenge?"

Once she accepted the fact that our presence boded her no harm, the whale showed a strange interest in us, almost as if she took pleasure in being close to our two 40-foot boats, whose undersides may have looked faintly whale-like in shape. Not only did she pass directly under us several times but she also passed between the two boats, carefully threading her way between our anchor cables. We had the distinct impression she was lonely—an impression shared by the Hann brothers when she hung close to their small boat. Claire went so far as to suggest the whale was seeking help, but how could we know about that?

I was greatly concerned about the effects of the gunning but, apart from a multitude of bullet holes, none of which showed signs of bleeding, she appeared to be in good health. Her movements were sure and powerful and there was no bloody discoloration in her blow. Because I so much wished to believe it, I concluded that the bullets had done no more harm than superficial damage and that, with luck, the great animal would be none the worse for her ordeal by fire.

At dusk we reluctantly left the Pond. Our communion with the whale had left all of us half hypnotized. We had almost nothing to say to each other until the R.C.M.P launch pulled alongside and Constable Murdoch shouted:

"There'll be no more shooting. I guarantee you that. Danny and me'll patrol every day from now on, and twice a day if we have to."

Murdoch's words brought me my first definite awareness of a decision which I must already have arrived at below—or perhaps above—the limited levels of conscious thought. As we headed back to Messers, I knew I was committed to the saving of that whale, as passionately as I had ever been committed to anything in my life. I still do not know why I felt such an instantaneous compulsion. Later it was possible to think of a dozen reasons, but these were afterthoughts—not reasons at the time. If I were a mystic, I might explain it by saying I had heard a call, and that may not be such a mad explanation after all. In the light of what ensued, it is not easy to dismiss the possibility that, in some incomprehensible way, alien flesh had reached out to alien flesh . . . cried out for help in a wordless and primordial appeal which could not be refused.

Farley Mowat's *love of nature awoke at the age of fourteen when he took a trip to the Arctic with his uncle, an ornithologist. Since then he has written more than two dozen books about people and nature, including* An Owl in the Family *and* Never Cry Wolf. *The tragic fate of the trapped fin whale is described in his book,* A Whale for the Killing, *from which this excerpt is drawn.*

Persistent Haiku

ELISAVIETTA RITCHIE

The hurricane past,
the spider returns
to lace up the shattered wharf.

Elisavietta Ritchie *has published eleven books of poetry and two of short fiction and also works as a poet-in-the-schools. She lives in Broome's Island, Maryland.*

The Legend of the Mashpee Maiden

Elizabeth Reynard

Chief Red Shell, Historian of the Nauset Wampanoag Tribe, and Chief Wild Horse, Wampanoag Champion of Mashpee, told the author this story and "generously contributed" it to her book The Narrow Land.

In the long ago, there lived among the Wampanoag of the Mashpee Village, a maiden called Ahsoo. Her legs were like pipe-stems; her chin was pointed and sharp as the beak of a loon; her nose was humped and crooked; and her eyes were as big as a frightened deer's. Day after day she sat on a log and watched those around her. No one cared for her; none of the men desired her friendship. She was an idle, lazy maiden who would not work in a wigwam nor carry wood for a fire.

Although Ahsoo was ugly, no woman could equal her in singing. Birds paused on the bough to listen to her, and the river, running over rapids, almost ceased its flowing to hear the Mashpee Maiden. On a low hill near the river Ahsoo would sit and sing. Beasts of the forest, birds of the air, fish of the lakes came to hear. Maugua the Bear came, and even the great War Eagle; but Ahsoo was not afraid for she knew that they had only come to listen to her songs. The river at the foot of the hill became alive with fishes, journeying up from the South Sea to hear the voice of Ahsoo. Every animal, bird, and fish applauded in its own manner, since they all greatly desired that Ahsoo should continue.

There was a big trout, chief of all trout, almost as big as a man. Because of his size he could not swim up the river to hear Ahsoo sing. Every night he burrowed his nose further and further into the bank. At length he planed a long path inland and the seawater, following him closely, made Cotuit Brook. This chief of the trout loved Ahsoo and he could not see how ugly she was, for she always sang in the summer evenings after the sun went down. So he told her that she was pretty; and of course the Mashpee Maiden fell deeply in love with that trout. She told him how she loved him and invited him to visit her wigwam.

At this time, the Pukwudgee chief lived with his followers in the marshes near Poponesset Bay. He observed the Great Trout who was making a new brook for the use of the pygmy people, and one day the little chief overheard the trout lamenting because he could not have Ahsoo for a wife.

"The charming Mashpee Maiden and I love each other dearly," sighed the Monster Fish, "but, alas! neither of us can live without the other, and neither of us can live where the other lives."

The chief of the Pukwudgees was sorry for these lovers, so he changed the Maiden into a trout, and placed her in Santuit Pond. Then he told the Monster Fish to dig his way to the Pond, and have the Maiden for his wife. The Trout digged so hard and so fast that, when he reached Santuit Pond, he died of too much exertion; and the Maiden who had become a trout died of a broken heart. Indians found the defeated lovers, and buried them side by side in a large mound, called *Trout Grave,* near the brook dug by the Chief of Trout.

Elizabeth Reynard *was born in Boston in 1896 and was an associate professor of literature at Barnard College for many years. When she had a home in Chatham, Massachusetts, she gathered material for her book* The Narrow Land, *in which this story appears.*

Fire Island Walking Song

EUGENE F. KINKEAD

I know a large dune rat whose first name is Joe
And he skips beneath the boardwalk medium slow
Out to the edge where the daylight glisters
And he hasn't any brothers and he hasn't any sisters
And he hasn't any uncles and he hasn't any aunts
And he hasn't any Sunday-go-to-meeting pants.

Oh, he lives all alone in the big tall grassages
And through the brush piles he has secret passages.
He dines on moonbeams and washed-up scobbles
And he never has the toothache or the collywobbles.
He comes out at night and he dances by the sea
And he's a pretty nice dune rat, if you're asking me.

Eugene F. Kinkead, *a longtime staff writer for the* New Yorker, *also wrote books on urban wildlife and Central Park.*

Waxwings

Henry Beetle Hough

Although winter months on Martha's Vineyard are wet and cold, cedar waxwings, chickadees, and many other plucky birds are willing to ruffle up their feathers and wait out the wintry weather.

It's quite a thing to have a flock of cedar waxwings paying you a visit in the calm of January, and not a few Vineyarders have had that experience.

Cedar waxwings are larger than chickadees and more svelte—an exotic word being best for exotic-looking birds like these—and they are not individualists in the same sense. Your chickadee is quite a citizen and maintains his own goings and comings, although he doesn't at all object to company. But the waxwings come in numbers, work in numbers, and go away in numbers.

They have unbelievable smoothness and neatness. They are lissome (that's what svelte means) and they wear black on their faces as if provided with dominoes for a winter masquerade. Their heads are crested, and their wings splashed with a bit of red like sealing wax, as the books say, and occasionally you see this red on their tails too. But the tips of their tails look as if they had been dipped in yellow paint. Waxwings manage to be spectacular without appearing garish, indeed without even being noticeable, if you can figure that out. Of course, if you've seen a winter flock of these birds and just barely missed not seeing them while glancing right at them, you can understand perfectly.

Waxwings feed on berries at this time of year—cedar berries, bittersweet berries, bayberries, and so on. They will whip in and out of a vine in no time, or they will drift about in twos and threes, grazing the garden, checking up on old seed pods and so on.

A winter in New England, and thus a winter on the Vineyard, should be an empty season (so Californians think) but there is so much to fill it and give it distinction. There's always the likelihood of snow, that bulky commodity, and meantime the cedar waxwings supply their precise and spirited accent to our by no means scanty scene.

Henry Beetle Hough *lived on Martha's Vineyard for almost all his life. The editor of the* Vineyard Gazette *for nearly sixty years, he also wrote more than twenty books and worked for environmental causes. In 1979 he received the Environmental Award from the Massachusetts Conservation Council.*

Germantown Friends Cemetery

YVONNE

Among the meek

stone teeth

grey squirrel twirls

a seed

Yvonne *is the author of a three-volume epic:* Iwilla Soil *(1985)*, Iwilla Scourge *(1986), and* Iwilla Rise *(1999). She was poetry editor at* Ms. *magazine from 1973–1986.*

A Moth Flies in Brooklyn

THOMAS J. CAMPANELLA

*Cities can be surprisingly good places for tracking and observing wildlife.
As Thomas Campanella discovered as a boy, the trick is patience and a
curiosity about even small wild lives.*

Were an official tree chosen for Brooklyn, the honor would no
doubt go to *Ailanthus altissima*—stinking ash, tree-of-heaven,
ghetto palm, the tenacious weed of Betty Smith's 1943 novel,
A Tree Grows in Brooklyn. As a child raised in the Flatlands section of the borough, I never had to wander far to come upon a
clump or specimen of ailanthus. Down by the Belt Parkway
was my favorite stand, a venerable grove that filled an entire
embankment near Exit Eleven, beside the Flatbush Avenue
overpass. The ailanthus there reached bravely and greenly sky-
ward, in spite of the carbon monoxide and road salt and the
indelicacies of highway maintenance crews. And these hardy
trees were, unbelievably, home to a vigorous population of
Samia cynthia—silk worms descended from creatures brought
to America in the late nineteenth century, in the hope of creat-
ing a native silk industry. The venture failed, but the worms
survived and their hosts gained a secure foothold in the new
land.

As an avid chaser of butterflies and moths, I was fascinated by *cynthia*. It was not just a lost rustic, but truly a child of the city. My beloved *Golden Nature Guide, Butterflies and Moths,* was quite clear on this: the *cynthia* moth, it said, is "found mostly near cities from Boston to Washington, D.C." (Its range has since spread, presumably along with that of the ailanthus; the latest edition of *Butterflies and Moths* describes the moth's territory as stretching "south to Savannah, and west to Indiana.") The *Audubon Society Guide to North American Insects and Spiders* delineated *cynthia's* domain as "Major metropolitan areas . . . where ailanthus is found." I had found a bit of urban nature that seemed in a different league than the starlings and pigeons and other common urban creatures. The *cynthia* moth was enigmatic, rarely seen, and remarkably beautiful.

One afternoon, I took several of the plump, horn-studded caterpillars home and placed them in an old dry fish tank. Every few days I would replenish their supply of ailanthus leaves, until one day I found that the caterpillars had tucked themselves into husklike brown cocoons. Several weeks passed, and then one morning my breath was taken away: the cocoons had opened. Dewy-winged *cynthia* moths were resting on the twigs, their discarded hatcheries nearby. The insects waited for the fluids in their plump bodies to pump wingward, to unfurl the powdery sheets like petals in the morning sun. Hours passed, and the big moths slowly took form. Their regal wings spread nearly five inches now, painted in pastel pinks and browns, marked with the beautiful, haunting "eyes" characteristic of the family Saturniidae. Fine antennae, like newly unfurled fern fronds, hung at their heads. It seemed decidedly uncouth to name these magnificent insects "moths"—a term that brought to mind holey winter woolens and the grandmotherly aroma of moth balls.

I kept them only long enough to show my parents and friends what had become of the "worms," and then I released them into the Brooklyn sky. There were six or seven moths I let fly that day, all females. But one I kept behind.

I had always been thrilled to find traces of nature in my city. A cardinal on a neighbor's fence, a wild pheasant in the

Gerritsen salt marshes, a flock of Canada geese hunkered down on the tawny March ballfields of Marine Park—these things I never expected to encounter as a Brooklyn child. When I did, nature, even in these wonderful forms, seemed reticent, on the defensive; it had to be searched out and flushed. And then, one night during the summer of the moths, nature in all its wild mystery came to me.

I had built a small cage for my last moth, from a section of coarse wire screen tacked to two wooden disks. That evening I took the cylindrical pen and placed it on a table in the garden. The moon silvered the staked tomatoes and pressed bold shadows of them into the russet brown garage wall. I sat and waited and watched, hoping that the newly emerged insect would attract a mate from the moonlit city sky. My *Golden Guide,* or some other trusty text, had hinted that such a thing would happen, that from as far as five miles away a mate would be called to join the female and together stoke the engines of life. As optimistic as I was, I suspected that the writers of my well-worn *Guides* had not Brooklyn (nor any city, for that matter) in mind when they wrote their evocative little essays.

I had fallen asleep on the chaise lounge in the backyard. My mother had placed a blanket on me and let me be with my moth. It was deeply quiet and still when I awoke; the moon was low and dim, but I could see in the pale of light that my companion was no longer alone. Through the wide gaps in the wire screen, the caged moth was locked in procreative embrace with a male she had lured out of the night sky. Her pheromones had conquered Brooklyn; a tiny bit of wildness had slipped into my presence, into this one small garden in the city. Led by its frondlike antennae, the visitor had glided over the tarred flat roofs of Flatlands, over the idling buses and parked cars, to be with my moth. It may have come from as far away as the Rockaways or Prospect Park, though I suspected it was just another lost child from Exit Eleven.

In the morning I set the last moth free. She would wander toward the ailanthus, I imagined, searching from a prospect high above the streets after the sun had gone down behind the row houses of south Brooklyn. Or maybe it was that the moth was simply heading home, guided by some unseen force to bed down her offspring in the rough grove by the acrid rush of the Belt Parkway.

Thomas J. Campanella *is an urbanist and cultural critic who has written about landscapes, cities, and the built environment around the world. He is currently completing a history of the American elm in New England, entitled* Republic of Shade.

Lunch with a Gull

VIRGINIA KROLL

I had lunch with a gull today.
It waddled up as if to say,
"Can you spare a bit of bread?"
It blinked its eyes and cocked its head.

We shared my sandwich and my pie.
We gladly gulped, the gull and I.
And afterward, we both took flight
With tummies heavy and hearts light.

Virginia Kroll *is the author of more than thirty books and sixteen hundred magazine articles for children. She lives in New York.*

Stranded

HENRY BESTON

In 1926, Henry Beston spent a year living in a small house he designed and built (and dubbed "the Fo'castle") on Coast Guard Beach in Eastham, Massachusetts. With only the crew of the nearby Nauset light-house for human company, Beston devoted most of his attention to the sea, the shore, and its many wild inhabitants. The following excerpt is taken from his account of that year, called The Outermost House.

On the next morning—it was sunny then, but still freezing cold—I chanced to go out for a moment to look at the marsh. About a mile and a half away, in one of the open channels, was a dark something which looked like a large, unfamiliar bird. A stray goose, perhaps? Taking my glass, I found the dark object to be the head of a deer swimming down the channel, and, even as I looked, there came to my ears the distant barking of dogs. A pair of marauding curs, out hunting on their own, had found a deer somewhere and driven the creature down the dunes and into the icy creeks. Down the channel it swam, and presently turned aside and climbed out on the marsh island just behind the Fo'castle. The animal was a young doe. I thought then, and I still believe, that this doe and the unseen creature whose delicate hoofprints I often found near the Fo'castle were one and the same. It lived, I believe, in the pines on the northern shore of the marsh and came down to the dunes at earliest dawn. But to return to its adventures: All afternoon I watched it standing on the island far out in the marsh, the tall, dead sea grass rising about its russet body; when night came, it was still there, a tiny spot of forlorn mammalian life in that frozen scene. Was it too terrified to return? That night a tide of unusual height was due which would submerge the islands under at least two feet of water and floating ice. Would the doe swim ashore under cover of darkness? I went out at midnight into my solitary world and saw the ice-covered marsh gleaming palely under a sky of brilliant stars, but could see nothing of the island or the doe save a ghostliness of salt ice along the nearer rim.

The first thing I did, on waking the next morning, was to search the island with my glass. The doe was still there.

I have often paused to wonder how that delicate and lovely creature endured so cruel a night, how she survived the slow rise of the icy tide about her poor legs, and the northwest gale that blustered about her all night long in that starlit loneliness of crunchy marsh mud and the murmur of the tides. The morning lengthened, the sun rose higher on the marsh, and presently the tide began to rise again. I watched it rising toward the refugee, and wondered if she could survive a second immersion. Just a little before noon, perhaps as the water was flooding round her feet, she came down to the edge of her island, and plunged into the channel. The creek was full of ice mush and of ice floes moving at a good speed; the doe was weak, the ice cakes bore down upon her, striking her heavily; she seemed confused, hesitated, swam here, swam there, stood still, and was struck cruelly by a floe which seemed to pass over her, yet on she swam, bewildered, but resolute for life. I had almost given up hope for her, when rescue came unexpectedly. My friend Bill Eldredge, it appeared, while on watch in the station tower the day before had chanced to see the beginning of the story, and on the second morning had noticed the doe still standing in the marshes. All the Nauset crew had taken an interest. Catching sight of the poor creature fighting for life in the drift, three of the men put off in a skiff, poled the ice away with their oars, and shepherded the doe ashore. "When she reached dry land, she couldn't rise, she was so weak, and fell down again and again. But finally she stood up and stayed up, and walked off into the pines."

Henry Beston *was born in Quincy, Massachusetts, in 1888. He attended Harvard College, served as a French volunteer in World War I, and lived on a farm in Maine for the last forty years of his life.*

Pickering Beach

MARYBETH RUA-LARSEN

Every spring, migrating shorebirds land on beaches along the Delaware
Bay just as thousands of horseshoe crabs are coming ashore to lay their
eggs. The birds feast on the eggs to fuel their long flights to the Arctic.
Sometimes the birds will feed on an overturned adult horseshoe crab,
too, but most of the horseshoes successfully lay their eggs and return to
the water unharmed.

When May invades Delaware's shore, hundreds
of horseshoe crabs litter this battlefield,
some empty helmets cradled by salty sand,
others with exposed belly wounds, too weary
to roll themselves over and crawl

to the sea. Thousands of red knots, rusty
breasts at attention, slop the crab's
jellied eggs while ruddy turnstones, allies
who scour nest sites, dig for rations.
Belligerent laughing gulls join the next wave

of attacks, and though a few crabs arm wrestle air
for leverage, they are unequipped for combat.
We turn over one crab, watch it circle

sand, tug itself toward the sea.
There are too many to rescue.

Knots and turnstones, bellies
bursting, mobilize long camouflaged wings
toward the Arctic. Horseshoe crabs
crackle in the sun.

Marybeth Rua-Larsen *teaches English at the Lancaster Campus of Harrisburg Area Community College in Pennsylvania. She credits her growth as a poet to her participation in the Feminist Women's Writing Workshop in Geneva, New York.*

Roostwatch

Marie Winn

One day, Marie Winn discovered the Central Park "Bird Register"—a notebook filled with handwritten comments about wildlife sightings throughout New York City's biggest park. Curious about these creatures and their human admirers, she introduced herself to Central Park's bird-watching community. Soon she was one of the "Regulars" who visited the park nearly every day. The following excerpt describes one of the group's many close-up encounters with their wild neighbors.

The stars were bright in the city sky as I left my house for Central Park. Yet none of the winter constellations were out, though it was February, not the brilliant-eyed Charioteer nor Orion the Hunter with his three-studded belt. And where was Sirius the Dog Star, brightest of all heavenly objects in the winter sky? The earth had spent the long night rotating on its axis and now, as I set off for Central Park at the unearthly hour of 5:00 a.m., the stars of a different season had risen in the winter sky: the giant star Arcturus as bright as a little moon overhead, and Altair, Vega, and Deneb, the great triangle of the summer sky, shining almost as radiantly as on an evening in July.

Not only the stars seem out of season when one is out in the city before dawn. There is a languid, almost tropical feel to the place at that hour, like Bogart's Key Largo before the hurricane strikes. You know that the storm is coming, that in an hour or two those hushed empty streets will be full of cars and trucks and taxis and buses with maddened drivers blasting their horns, trading insults about each other's mothers and fathers; you know that those empty sidewalks will be full of people bumping into each other while failing to apologize. All hell is about to break loose, but at five in the morning the storm seems far away.

The streets were almost deserted as I walked toward my destination that morning: only a newspaper delivery man removing bundles from a car trunk, a doorman smoking outside an apartment house, and an old man sweeping in front of an all-night grocery to give a hint of the workaday world. Here and there another passerby, someone coming home from somewhere—a night of illicit love, an all-night vigil at a deathbed; someone on the way to somewhere—a train to catch, an early shift as short-order cook at a Greek coffee shop. I caught myself staring at one of those dawn walkers, wondering why he was out at such an hour, what his story was. I laughed to think what he'd say if he knew mine.

It began a few weeks earlier, on a freezing Sunday afternoon in January as Norma Collin was making her daily rounds of the Ramble. That's when she heard a loud tattoo coming from a nearby tree.

"I know that sound," she thought cheerfully, and within minutes she had found her bird: a downy woodpecker, the smaller and more common of Central Park's two resident woodpeckers (the red-bellied is the other, though a few hairy woodpeckers and flickers sometimes overwinter). The little bird was in a half-dead black cherry tree, drilling away at a short, stubby snag about ten feet from the ground.

The woodpecker was familiar, but its action was puzzling. It was not just drumming as woodpeckers often do, sending a message of love or war to another of its kind, nor was it extracting larvae or grubs from crevices in the bark. It was clearly making a hole.

Clinging to the reddish-brown, scaly bark with feet especially adapted for feeding on vertical surfaces—two toes pointing forward and two back—zygodactyl is the scientific term—while bracing itself with its stiffened, spinelike tail feathers, the woodpecker attacked the branch with a steady, rapid back-and-forth motion. It looked for all the world like a living black-and-white jackhammer. The cavity was already quite deep, and every so often the bird would briefly disappear within for a second or two, and then reappear to toss out billful after billful of sawdust, with a jaunty flick of its head at each toss.

What in the world is this bird up to? Norma wondered. It wasn't odd to see a woodpecker making a hole exactly the way this one was doing. But that was to be expected at the start of the breeding season, in April or May. Why was this bird excavating a hole in January? As she watched, she noted that the woodpecker was definitely a *he:* on the back of his head was a bright red patch, the only feature that distinguishes male downies from females. Well, maybe he's practicing for spring, she finally decided, and left it at that.

Norma had been observing the woodpecker for a good fifteen minutes and her fingers and toes were numb. She was looking forward to getting home and settling down with a nice cup of linden tea—she had picked the blossoms herself from a tree on Pilgrim Hill the previous spring. First, however, a quick stop at the Boathouse to write down her day's sightings in the Bird Register. During the excitement of the migration seasons a bird like a downy woodpecker is hardly even mentioned in the long lists of visitors that fill the Register's pages. But January is a month when the park's residents—woodpeckers, sparrows, blue jays, crows, titmice, and cardinals—take center stage. The downy woodpecker drilling a hole near lamppost 7631 was by far the most important sighting Norma had to report that day.

The next day Charles Kennedy, voracious reader of bird books and accumulator of arcane information about almost any natural history subject, came up with a possible explanation. He happened to have, among his huge number of bird books, one called *Woodpeckers of Eastern North America* written by an engaging amateur naturalist named Lawrence Kilham. That's where Charles got the idea that Norma's woodpecker must have been making a winter roost hole.

Roost holes, according to Kilham, offer a woodpecker insulation against cold and shelter from the wind. When the outside temperature is 17 degrees Fahrenheit it can be 11 degrees higher inside a roost hole, even higher if the woodpecker's body fits the cavity exactly. "The amount of energy . . . conserved may make the difference between survival and death during periods of extreme weather during winter," Kilham wrote.

A woodpecker's winter roost hole has advantages for bird-watchers as well: it offers anyone wishing to study the Picidae family an opportunity to locate its members dependably. "Just wait until an hour after sunrise, and the chances of locating a Downy or a Hairy in a reasonable time can be slim. . . . But in taking the trouble to be by a roost hole at dawn, I have had some of the best of birdwatching," wrote Kilham.

Yes! thought Charles, lover of eccentric projects. If Norma's discovery turns out to be a roost hole, we've got some serious woodpecker-studying to do.

It was almost 5:30 a.m. on that February morning by the time I arrived at Naturalists Gate, the park entrance at West 77th Street. The other five birdwatchers were already waiting and we entered the park at once. Though it was almost an hour before sunrise, day was beginning to break, and we didn't want to be late. Crossing the Upper Lobe at Bank Rock Bridge, we took a short path going south, and then east, taking us under the Rustic Arch with its buttresses of natural stone. Then we were in the woods, in the wilds of the Ramble.

A few moments later we arrived at the scraggly cherry tree. There we put down our knapsacks, took out our thermoses of coffee, and settled in for a wait. Roostwatch had officially begun.

The woods were silent and the roost hole was barely visible in the semi-darkness. Good. We'd arrived in time—every bird in the park was still asleep. Now we would keep a watch to see if a downy woodpecker was roosting within.

We waited and watched the day grow brighter. Around 6:00 a.m. we heard the first bird sounds—blue jays screaming in the distance. The roost hole was silent. Sunrise arrived at 6:24 a.m.—no sign of life at the cherry tree snag.

In truth, few of us had faith that there was a bird inside that neat hole, not even Charles, who is a dyed-in-the-wool optimist. I wasn't convinced that there even *was* such a thing as a roost hole, in spite of Kilham. After all, there had been downy woodpeckers in Central Park for as long as anyone could remember. Wouldn't someone have seen a roost hole by this time—Tom Fiore, for instance? And yet we must have had more than a little room for hope. Why else would we have been willing to spend all that time standing and waiting, our toes and fingertips freezing and puffs of smoke coming out of our mouths with every breath as the temperature hovered around 20 degrees?

Our little band waited on. If you get up at 4:15 in the morning you don't give up just like that. At 6:40 a.m. Charles said rather quietly: "Well, look who's there." The rest of us were deep in conversation. We looked up and saw a soft, fuzzy head filling up the roost hole entrance. The bird was decidedly morning-sleepy.

First the woodpecker stared straight ahead without moving, as if in a trance. After a minute or two he began to look up and down and up and down, more alert. Finally he seemed to fix his gaze directly at us. "What? You guys?" I imagined him thinking. "I have to put up with the sight of you and your binoculars all day long in the park. Now you're here when I get up in the morning too!"

He flew out—whoosh! It happened so fast we couldn't entirely believe what we'd seen. Was it a group delusion? No, everyone finally agreed, we had really seen a bird zip out of the hole. Charles looked at his watch. It was exactly 6:42 a.m.

The woodpecker alighted on a nearby dead branch and commenced a loud tattoo, a long unbroken drumroll. There were ten bursts of drumming, which Charles diligently timed. Each lasted about six seconds. Experts can identify a woodpecker by its drum pattern. The hairy woodpecker's roll is shorter and louder than a downy's, with a greater interval between each stroke. The yellow-bellied sapsucker starts with a short roll and ends with five or six distinct taps. Sapsuckers, by the way, appear in Central Park only during migration. Their grid-like rows of neat holes (for collecting sap) may be seen on the trunks of many park trees.

An active roost hole! Usually the excitement of birdwatching is based on unpredictability, for unpredictability breeds hope. As you stroll around with binoculars at the ready, you never know when something new and exciting, perhaps something rare or beautiful might show up. That's hope.

Now the pleasure was in the very predictability of the bird. Predictability breeds hope too, we discovered, the same sort of hope that each year's cycle of seasons inspires. It is somehow deeply fulfilling and hopeful to know that the phoebe will arrive in Central Park on March 13th every year, give or take a few days. Or that if you stand at a certain place at a certain time a particular bird will show up and perform a predictable action—like zipping in or out of a hole in a tree.

A small group of Regulars began to monitor the roost hole with regularity, both at dawn and at sunset when the bird flew in for the night. The essence of Roostwatch was timekeeping, making note of the bird's precise moment of entry and exit. This produced a fact, a concrete piece of data. Charles Kennedy, the major instigator of the project, loved facts. Above all he loved to time. He timed how long cardinals bathed in his brook under Balcony Bridge. He timed owl fly-outs, and mockingbird songs. He also loved to measure—the sticks in the ill-fated hawk nest, for example.

On March 16th, with an orange-red full moon setting in the west just before sunrise, woodpecker wake-up was at 6:01 a.m. On the evening of March 27th and the following morning, March 28th, the roostwatchers managed to document a woodpecker's full night of sleep. They watched the bird scoot in at 5:55 p.m. They returned the next morning—it hardly seemed worth going home, somebody quipped—and observed downy reveille: it was 5:46 a.m., one minute before sunrise. The bird had been in the roost hole for eleven hours and fifty-one minutes, Charles Kennedy announced.

On April 9th, a cold spring day, a new development at the early morning Roostwatch warmed the watchers' hearts if not their toes. A moment or two after the woodpecker emerged from his roost hole at 6:38 a.m. (the bird was not sleeping in that morning—Daylight Savings Time had commenced), another downy woodpecker materialized as if out of nowhere. Double vision. Only one bird had flown out of the hole, and now there were two woodpeckers climbing on a nearby branch. They looked identical but for one detail: no red patch on the newcomer's head. It was a female. "Yahoo!" exclaimed Charles, the eternal romantic.

After that, the female showed up regularly at Roostwatch, morning and evening. Before bedtime the two birds were often seen feeding in the vicinity, busily working the bark of nearby trunks and branches for whatever it is that woodpeckers extract from crevices—seeds, bugs, larvae. Then, as night began to fall the female would fly off somewhere—to her own roost hole, no doubt—and he would zip into his. In the morning the female was often on a nearby tree, waiting for her sweetheart to rise and shine.

April 28th was a warm, balmy spring day. Six roostwatchers had assembled for the evening roostwatch by 6:30 p.m. This time they did not reminisce about past vigils at the roost hole, those cold February and March waits. Tonight the talk was about the present, about the day's birds.

Spring migration was in full swing and the day had been a

glorious one: scarlet tanagers, rose-breasted grosbeaks, an orchard oriole, and a yellow-billed cuckoo had been sighted in the Ramble. Tom Fiore had heard a singing indigo bunting at 6:20 a.m. that very morning. The electric blue bird had been near the Belvedere Castle at the same place indigo buntings show up every year—near a patch of Kentucky bluegrass favored by that species. Tom had also sighted a least flycatcher making his "che-bek che-bek" call, the only way you can distinguish this bird from four other small, virtually identical flycatchers. Nineteen species of warblers had been seen so far that spring, and Tom had seen sixteen that very day.

Little leaves were already out on the scraggly cherry; soon they would obscure the roost hole. Somebody picked one and crushed it to demonstrate its bitter smell—cyanide! That evening the woodpecker took the longest time arriving.

He didn't show up until 7:30 p.m., later than ever before. The female arrived almost immediately after. The pair first flew from branch to branch of a nearby tree, making little chip sounds and feeding desultorily. At about 7:35 the female suddenly disappeared, and at 7:43—whoop!—into the hole whizzed the male. This time there was a round of applause from the assembled gang.

Night had fallen and the Regulars walked out of the park together. No matter how many times it had happened before, it still seemed incredible, incredible to have penetrated the secret life of a creature so *other*.

On the morning of May 3rd four watchers waited from 5:30 a.m. to 7:00 a.m. We waited and waited until the day was bright and clear, as clear as our knowledge that no bird was going to come out of the hole. Quite a few other birds showed up in the vicinity that morning—a great crested flycatcher and a wood thrush singing its enchanting song. Also seven species of warblers. Everything was lush and green. The knotweed was high as an elephant's eye. But the roost hole was empty.

The downy woodpecker and his mate failed to show up at the roost hole that evening, and the next. Gone. Obviously they had other business to take care of. This had been a winter roost hole, after all, and the winter was over.

Marie Winn *has published thirteen books and writes a column on nature and bird-watching for the* Wall Street Journal. *She spends part of every day in Central Park.*

Today

NADYA AISENBERG

Sailing home from the Barred Islands today
we saw two dolphins in tandem flash
That was enough for today
And tomorrow

Nadya Aisenberg *was an adjunct associate professor of women's studies at Brandeis University in Boston, Massachusetts, and the author of four nonfiction books.*

A White Heron

Sarah Orne Jewett

Written in the late 1800s, this story describes the widespread practice of collecting animal specimens for study or museum display. While such collecting has helped advance our understanding of biology and taxonomy, the practice is now highly regulated to protect wild species, especially rare ones. The white heron described in this story is probably a snowy egret, a bird that was nearly hunted to extinction by the end of the nineteenth century but that is now quite common throughout its range.

One

The woods were already filled with shadows one June evening, just before eight o'clock, though a bright sunset still glimmered faintly among the trunks of the trees. A little girl was driving home her cow, a plodding, dilatory, provoking creature in her behavior, but a valued companion for all that. They were going away from the western light, and striking deep into the dark woods, but their feet were familiar with the path, and it was no matter whether their eyes could see it or not.

There was hardly a night the summer through when the old cow could be found waiting at the pasture bars; on the contrary, it was her greatest pleasure to hide herself away among the high huckleberry bushes, and though she wore a loud bell she had made the discovery that if one stood perfectly still it would not ring. So Sylvia had to hunt for her until she found her, and call Co'! Co'! with never an answering Moo, until her childish patience was quite spent. If the creature had not given good milk and plenty of it, the case would have seemed very different to her owners. Besides, Sylvia had all the time there was, and very little use to make of it. Sometimes in pleasant weather it was a consolation to look upon the cow's pranks as an intelligent attempt to play hide and seek, and as the child had no playmates she lent herself to this amusement with a good deal of zest. Though this chase had been so long that the wary animal herself had given an unusual signal of her whereabouts, Sylvia had only laughed when she came upon Mistress Moolly at the swamp-side, and urged her affectionately homeward with a twig of birch leaves. The old cow was not inclined to wander farther, she even turned in the right direction for once as they left the pasture, and stepped along the road at a good pace. She was quite ready to be milked now, and seldom stopped to browse. Sylvia wondered what her grandmother would say because they were so late. It was a great while since she had left home at half past five o'clock, but everybody knew the difficulty of making this errand a short one. Mrs. Tilley had chased the hornéd torment too many summer evenings herself to blame any one else for lingering, and was only thankful as she waited that she had Sylvia, nowadays, to give such valuable assistance. The good woman suspected that Sylvia loitered occasionally on her own account; there never was such a child for straying about out-of-doors since the world was made! Everybody said that it was a good change for a little maid who had tried to grow for eight years in a crowded manufacturing town, but, as for Sylvia herself, it seemed as if she never had been alive at all before she came to live at the farm. She thought often with wistful compassion of a wretched dry geranium that belonged to a town neighbor.

"'Afraid of folks,'" old Mrs. Tilley said to herself, with a smile, after she had made the unlikely choice of Sylvia from her daughter's houseful of children, and was returning to the farm. "'Afraid of folks,' they said! I guess she won't be troubled no great with 'em up to the old place!" When they reached the door of the lonely house and stopped to unlock it, and the cat came to purr loudly, and rub against them, a deserted pussy, indeed, but fat with young robins, Sylvia whispered that this was a beautiful place to live in, and she never should wish to go home.

The companions followed the shady woodroad, the cow taking slow steps, and the child very fast ones. The cow stopped long at the brook to drink, as if the pasture were not half a swamp, and Sylvia stood still and waited, letting her bare feet cool themselves in the shoal water, while the great twilight moths struck softly against her. She waded on through the brook as the cow moved away, and listened to the thrushes with a heart that beat fast with pleasure. There was a stirring in the great boughs overhead. They were full of little birds and beasts that seemed to be wide-awake, and going about their world, or else saying goodnight to each other in sleep twitters. Sylvia herself felt sleepy as she walked along. However, it was not much farther to the house, and the air was soft and sweet. She was not often in the woods so late as this, and it made her feel as if she were a part of the gray shadows and the moving leaves. She was just thinking how long it seemed since she first came to the farm a year ago, and wondering if everything went on in the noisy town just the same as when she was there; the thought of the great red-faced boy who used to chase and frighten her made her hurry along the path to escape from the shadow of the trees.

Suddenly this little woods-girl is horror-stricken to hear a clear whistle not very far away. Not a bird's whistle, which would have a sort of friendliness, but a boy's whistle, determined, and somewhat aggressive. Sylvia left the cow to whatever sad fate might await her, and stepped discreetly aside into the bushes, but she was just too late. The enemy had discovered her, and called out in a very cheerful and persuasive tone, "Halloa, little girl, how far is it to the road?" and trembling Sylvia answered almost inaudibly, "A good ways."

She did not dare to look boldly at the tall young man, who carried a gun over his shoulder, but she came out of her bush and again followed the cow, while he walked alongside.

"I have been hunting for some birds," the stranger said kindly, "and I have lost my way, and need a friend very much. Don't be afraid," he added gallantly. "Speak up and tell me what your name is, and whether you think I can spend the night at your house, and go out gunning early in the morning."

Sylvia was more alarmed than before. Would not her grandmother consider her much to blame? But who could have foreseen such an accident as this? It did not appear to be her fault, and she hung her head as if the stem of it were broken, but managed to answer "Sylvy," with much effort when her companion again asked her name.

Mrs. Tilley was standing in the doorway when the trio came into view. The cow gave a loud moo by way of explanation.

"Yes, you'd better speak up for yourself, you old trial! Where'd she tuck herself away this time, Sylvy?" Sylvia kept an awed silence; she knew by instinct that her grandmother did not comprehend the gravity of the situation. She must be mistaking the stranger for one of the farmer-lads of the region.

The young man stood his gun beside the door, and dropped a heavy game-bag beside it; then he bade Mrs. Tilley good-evening, and repeated his wayfarer's story, and asked if he could have a night's lodging.

"Put me anywhere you like," he said. "I must be off early in the morning, before day; but I am very hungry, indeed. You can give me some milk at any rate, that's plain."

"Dear sakes, yes," responded the hostess, whose long slumbering hospitality seemed to be easily awakened. "You might fare better if you went out on the main road a mile or so, but you're welcome to what we've got. I'll milk right off, and you make yourself at home. You can sleep on husks or feathers," she proffered graciously. "I raised them all myself. There's good pasturing for geese just below here towards the ma'sh. Now step round and set a plate for the gentleman, Sylvy!" And Sylvia promptly stepped. She was glad to have something to do, and she was hungry herself.

It was a surprise to find so clean and comfortable a little dwelling in this New England wilderness. The young man had known the horrors of its most primitive housekeeping, and the dreary squalor of that level of society which does not rebel at the companionship of hens. This was the best thrift of an old-fashioned farmstead, though on such a small scale that it seemed like a hermitage. He listened eagerly to the old woman's quaint talk, he watched Sylvia's pale face and shining gray eyes with ever growing enthusiasm, and insisted that this was the best supper he had eaten for a month; then, afterward, the new-made friends sat down in the doorway together while the moon came up.

Soon it would be berry-time, and Sylvia was a great help at picking. The cow was a good milker, though a plaguy thing to keep track of, the hostess gossiped frankly, adding presently that she had buried four children, so that Sylvia's mother, and a son (who might be dead) in California were all the children she had left. "Dan, my boy, was a great hand to go gunning," she explained sadly. "I never wanted for pa'tridges or gray squer'ls while he was to home. He's been a great wand'rer, I expect, and he's no hand to write letters. There, I don't blame him, I'd ha' seen the world myself if it had been so I could.

"Sylvia takes after him," the grandmother continued affectionately, after a minute's pause. "There ain't a foot o' ground she don't know her way over, and the wild creatur's counts her one o' themselves. Squer'ls she'll tame to come an' feed right out o' her hands, and all sorts o' birds. Last winter she got the jay-birds to bangeing here, and I believe she'd 'a' scanted herself of her own meals to have plenty to throw out amongst 'em, if I hadn't kep' watch. Anything but crows, I tell her, I'm willin' to help support,—though Dan he went an' tamed one o' them that did seem to have reason same as folks. It was round here a good spell after he went away. Dan an' his father they didn't hitch,—but he never held up his head ag'in after Dan had dared him an' gone off."

The guest did not notice this hint of family sorrows in his eager interest in something else.

"So Sylvy knows all about birds, does she?" he exclaimed, as he looked round at the little girl who sat, very demure but increasingly sleepy, in the moonlight. "I am making a collection of birds myself. I have been at it ever since I was a boy." (Mrs. Tilley smiled.) "There are two or three very rare ones I have been hunting for these five years. I mean to get them on my own ground if they can be found."

"Do you cage 'em up?" asked Mrs. Tilley doubtfully, in response to this enthusiastic announcement.

"Oh, no, they're stuffed and preserved, dozens and dozens of them," said the ornithologist, "and I have shot or snared every one myself. I caught a glimpse of a white heron three miles from here on Saturday, and I have followed it in this direction. They have never been found in this district at all. The little white heron, it is," and he turned again to look at Sylvia with hope of discovering that the rare bird was one of her acquaintances.

But Sylvia was watching a hop-toad in the narrow footpath.

"You would know the heron if you saw it," the stranger continued eagerly. "A queer tall white bird with soft feathers and long thin legs. And it would have a nest perhaps in the top of a high tree, made of sticks, something like a hawk's nest."

Sylvia's heart gave a wild beat; she knew that strange white bird, and had once stolen softly near where it stood in some bright green swamp grass, away over at the other side of the woods. There was an open place where the sunshine always seemed strangely yellow and hot, where tall, nodding rushes grew, and her grandmother had warned her that she might sink in the soft black mud underneath and never be heard of more. Not far beyond were the salt marshes and beyond those was the sea, the sea which Sylvia wondered and dreamed about, but never had looked upon, though its great voice could often be heard above the noise of the woods on stormy nights.

"I can't think of anything I should like so much as to find that heron's nest," the handsome stranger was saying. "I would give ten dollars to anybody who could show it to me," he added desperately, "and I mean to spend my whole vacation hunting for it if need be. Perhaps it was only migrating, or had been chased out of its own region by some bird of prey."

Mrs. Tilley gave amazed attention to all this, but Sylvia still watched the toad, not divining, as she might have done at some calmer time, that the creature wished to get to its hole under the doorstep, and was much hindered by the unusual spectators at that hour of the evening. No amount of thought, that night, could decide how many wished-for treasures the ten dollars, so lightly spoken of, would buy.

The next day the young sportsman hovered about the woods, and Sylvia kept him company, having lost her first fear of the friendly lad, who proved to be most kind and sympathetic. He told her many things about the birds and what they knew and where they lived and what they did with themselves. And he gave her a jack-knife, which she thought as great a treasure as if she were a desert-islander. All day long he did not once make her troubled or afraid except when he brought down some unsuspecting singing creature from its bough. Sylvia would have liked him vastly better without his gun; she could not understand why he killed the very birds he seemed to like so much. But as the day waned, Sylvia still watched the young man with loving admiration. She had never seen anybody so charming and delightful; the woman's heart, asleep in the child, was vaguely thrilled by a dream of love. Some premonition of that great power stirred and swayed these young foresters who traversed the solemn woodlands with soft-footed silent care. They stopped to listen to a bird's song; they pressed forward again eagerly, parting the branches,—speaking to each other rarely and in whispers; the young man going first and Sylvia following, fascinated, a few steps behind, with her gray eyes dark with excitement.

She grieved because the longed-for white heron was elusive, but she did not lead the guest, she only followed, and there was no such thing as speaking first. The sound of her own unquestioned voice would have terrified her,—it was hard enough to answer yes or no when there was need of that. At last evening began to fall, and they drove the cow home together, and Sylvia smiled with pleasure when they came to the place where she heard the whistle and was afraid only the night before.

Two

Half a mile from home, at the farther edge of the woods, where the land was highest, a great pine-tree stood, the last of its generation. Whether it was left for a boundary mark, or for what reason, no one could say; the woodchoppers who had felled its mates were dead and gone long ago, and a whole forest of sturdy trees, pines and oaks and maples, had grown again. But the stately head of this old pine towered above them all and made a landmark for sea and shore miles and miles away. Sylvia knew it well. She had always believed that whoever climbed to the top of it could see the ocean; and the little girl had often laid her hand on the great rough trunk and looked up wistfully at those dark boughs that the wind always stirred, no matter how hot and still the air might be below. Now she thought of the tree with a new excitement, for why, if one climbed it at break of day, could not one see all the world, and easily discover whence the white heron flew, and mark the place, and find the hidden nest?

What a spirit of adventure, what wild ambition! What fancied triumph and delight and glory for the later morning when she could make known the secret! It was almost too real and too great for the childish heart to bear.

All night the door of the little house stood open, and the whippoorwills came and sang upon the very step. The young sportsman and his old hostess were sound asleep, but Sylvia's great design kept her broad awake and watching. She forgot to think of sleep. The short summer night seemed as long as the winter darkness, and at last when the whippoorwills ceased, and she was afraid the morning would after all come too soon, she stole out of the house and followed the pasture path through the woods, hastening toward the open ground beyond, listening with a sense of comfort and companionship to the drowsy twitter of a half-awakened bird, whose perch she had jarred in passing. Alas, if the great wave of human interest which flooded for the first time this dull little life should sweep away the satisfactions of an existence heart to heart with nature and the dumb life of the forest!

There was the huge tree asleep yet in the paling moonlight, and small and hopeful Sylvia began with utmost bravery to mount to the top of it, with tingling, eager blood coursing the channels of her whole frame, with her bare feet and fingers, that pinched and held like bird's claws to the monstrous ladder reaching up, up, almost to the sky itself. First she must mount the white oak tree that grew alongside, where she was almost lost among the dark branches and the green leaves heavy and wet with dew; a bird fluttered off its nest, and a red squirrel ran to and fro and scolded pettishly at the harmless housebreaker. Sylvia felt her way easily. She had often climbed there, and knew that higher still one of the oak's upper branches chafed against the pine trunk, just where its lower boughs were set close together. There, when she made the dangerous pass from one tree to the other, the great enterprise would really begin.

She crept out along the swaying oak limb at last, and took the daring step across into the old pine-tree. The way was harder than she thought; she must reach far and hold fast, the sharp dry twigs caught and held her and scratched her like angry talons, the pitch made her thin little fingers clumsy and stiff as she went round and round the tree's great stem, higher and higher upward. The sparrows and robins in the woods below were beginning to wake and twitter to the dawn, yet it seemed much lighter there aloft in the pine-tree, and the child knew that she must hurry if her project were to be of any use.

The tree seemed to lengthen itself out as she went up, and to reach farther and farther upward. It was like a great mainmast to the voyaging earth; it must truly have been amazed that morning through all its ponderous frame as it felt this determined spark of human spirit creeping and climbing from higher branch to branch. Who knows how steadily the least twigs held themselves to advantage this light, weak creature on her way! The old pine must have loved his new dependent. More than all the hawks, and bats, and moths, and even the sweet-voiced thrushes, was the brave, beating heart of the solitary gray-eyed child. And the tree stood still and held away the winds that June morning while the dawn grew bright in the east.

Sylvia's face was like a pale star, if one had seen it from the ground, when the last thorny bough was past, and she stood trembling and tired but wholly triumphant, high in the tree-top. Yes, there was the sea with the dawning sun making a golden dazzle over it, and toward that glorious east flew two hawks with slow-moving pinions. How low they looked in the air from that height when before one had only seen them far up, and dark against the blue sky. Their gray feathers were as soft as moths; they seemed only a little way from the tree, and Sylvia felt as if she too could go flying away among the clouds. Westward, the woodlands and farms reached miles and miles into the distance; here and there were church steeples, and white villages; truly it was a vast and awesome world.

The birds sang louder and louder. At last the sun came up bewilderingly bright. Sylvia could see the white sails of ships out at sea, and the clouds that were purple and rose-colored and yellow at first began to fade away. Where was the white heron's nest in the sea of green branches, and was this wonderful sight and pageant of the world the only reward for having climbed to such a giddy height? Now look down again, Sylvia, where the green marsh is set among the shining birches and dark hemlocks; there where you saw the white heron once you will see him again; look, look! a white spot of him like a single floating feather comes up from the dead hemlock and grows larger, and rises, and comes close at last, and goes by the land-mark pine with steady sweep of wing and outstretched slender neck and crested head. And wait! wait! do not move a foot or a finger, little girl, do not send an arrow of light and conscious-ness from your two eager eyes, for the heron has perched on a pine bough not far beyond yours, and cries back to his mate on the nest, and plumes his feathers for the new day!

The child gives a long sigh and a minute later when a com-pany of shouting cat-birds comes also to the tree, and vexed by their fluttering and lawlessness the solemn heron goes away. She knows his secret now, the wild, light, slender bird that floats and wavers, and goes back like an arrow presently to his home in the green world beneath. Then Sylvia, well satisfied, makes her perilous way down again, not daring to look far below the branch she stands on, ready to cry sometimes because her fingers ache and her lamed feet slip. Wondering over and over again what the stranger would say to her, and what he would think when she told him how to find his way straight to the heron's nest.

"Sylvy, Sylvy!" called the busy old grandmother again and again, but nobody answered, and the small husk bed was empty, and Sylvia had disappeared.

The guest waked from a dream, and remembering his day's pleasure hurried to dress himself that it might sooner begin. He was sure from the way the shy little girl looked once or twice yesterday that she had at least seen the white heron, and now she must really be persuaded to tell. Here she comes now, paler than ever, and her worn old frock is torn and tattered, and smeared with pine pitch. The grandmother and the sportsman stand in the door together and question her, and the splendid moment has come to speak of the dead hemlock-tree by the green marsh.

But Sylvia does not speak after all, though the old grandmother fretfully rebukes her, and the young man's kind appealing eyes are looking straight in her own. He can make them rich with money; he has promised it, and they are poor now. He is so well worth making happy, and he waits to hear the story she can tell.

No, she must keep silence! What is it that suddenly forbids

her and makes her dumb? Has she been nine years growing, and now, when the great world for the first time puts out a hand to her, must she thrust it aside for a bird's sake? The murmur of the pine's green branches is in her ears, she remembers how the white heron came flying through the golden air and how they watched the sea and the morning together, and Sylvia cannot speak; she cannot tell the heron's secret and give its life away.

Dear loyalty, that suffered a sharp pang as the guest went away disappointed later in the day, that could have served and followed him and loved him as a dog loves! Many a night Sylvia heard the echo of his whistle haunting the pasture path as she came home with the loitering cow. She forgot even her sorrow at the sharp report of his gun and the piteous sight of thrushes and sparrows dropping silent to the ground, their songs hushed and their pretty feathers stained and wet with blood. Were the birds better friends than their hunter might have been,—who can tell? Whatever treasures were lost to her, woodlands and summer-time, remember! Bring your gifts and graces and tell your secrets to this lonely country child!

Sarah Orne Jewett *was born in 1840 in South Berwick, Maine, where she lived for most of her life. She published fourteen collections of stories, several volumes of verse, and a number of children's books before her death in 1909.*

Appendixes

❧

Ecology of the
North Atlantic Coast

What Is an Ecoregion?

The *Stories from Where We Live* series celebrates the literature of North America's diverse *ecoregions*. Ecoregions are large geographic areas that share similar climate, soils, and plant and animal communities. Thinking ecoregionally helps us understand how neighboring cities and states are connected and makes it easier for people to coordinate the use and protection of shared rivers, forests, watersheds, mountain ranges, and other natural areas. For our part, we believe that ecoregions provide an illuminating way to organize and compare place-based literature.

While many institutions have mapped the world's ecoregions, no existing delineation of ecoregions (or similar unit, such as *provinces* or *bioregions*) proved perfectly suited to a literary series. We created our own set of ecoregions based largely on existing scientific designations, with an added consideration for regional differences in human culture.

NORTHWEST

PACIFIC

COAST

THE

BOREAL

ROCKY MOUNTAINS

GREAT

NORTH

CALIFORNIA

COAST

WESTERN

DESERTS

AND

PLATEAUS

HAWAIIAN

ISLANDS

ARCTIC

FOREST

GREAT LAKES

NORTHEAST WOODLANDS

NORTH ATLANTIC COAST

AMERICAN PRAIRIE

APPALACHIAN HIGHLANDS

SOUTH ATLANTIC COAST AND PIEDMONT

SOUTHERN HILL COUNTRY

GULF COAST

Defining the
North Atlantic Coast

Scientists have lots of ways of parceling out the North Atlantic Coast into manageable pieces. If you're a toe-dipping sort, you might appreciate knowing that water temperatures are noticeably colder north of Cape Cod, Massachusetts, than south of it. And water temperatures north of Cape Hatteras, North Carolina, are much colder than those to the south. The result is three distinct zones of water temperature. Some species of plants and animals are uniquely suited to just one or two of these zones; others can tolerate a range of water temperatures.

If you're a beachgoer, you may have observed another natural boundary along the North Atlantic Coast: the beaches from New York northward (not including Cape Cod and the islands) are generally rockier than the beaches to the south. That's because glaciers that advanced from the north more than twelve thousand years ago got no farther than New York City. Even though the glaciers are long gone, rocky shores are part of the enduring rubble they left behind.

Based solely on these two pieces of information, one might expect the southern boundary of our ecoregion to end with Cape Cod, New York, or Cape Hatteras. But that's where culture comes in. Delaware is generally more closely aligned with the culture of the northern states; after all, the Mason-Dixon line divides it from Maryland to the south and west. So, for that reason, our ecoregion extends south to the Delaware Bay.

Where that takes us is from the cold waters of Newfoundland, past the green hills of Prince Edward Island and the spruce-lined shores of New Brunswick and Nova Scotia, bumping along Maine's rocky coast, past New Hampshire's brief stretch of shoreline, around the arm of Cape Cod where oaks and pitch pine become more common, in and out of the inlets of Rhode Island, then winding west past the salt marshes and salt ponds of Connecticut, south to Manhattan and the barrier beaches of Long Island, along New Jersey's sandy shores, and slipping around the Delaware Bay to the eastern edge of the Delmarva Peninsula.

As large and diverse as this area is, its history, economy, and life-forms have all been shaped by the Atlantic Ocean is some way. Think fish, for example. Early Beothuk, Micmac, Wampanoag, and other native groups relied on the seas as a regular source of food. Sometime around 1000 A.D., Atlantic fisheries lured the first Viking ships from Iceland and Greenland over to the Newfoundland coast. Later, new methods of drying fish over fires prompted fishermen from Portugal, England, and other countries to set up seasonal camps on shore, leading the way for European exploration and settlement. Fish even played a key role in the life of the Pilgrims, who probably would not have survived their first winter if Chief Squanto hadn't taught them to catch shellfish, eels, and shad. Fish have given us place names—Alewife Brook, Cape Cod, and Halibut Beach, to name a few. And despite some serious declines in Atlantic fisheries, fish and shellfish continue to boost the economy of all the states and provinces that border the Atlantic, especially the Canadian Maritimes, Maine, Massachusetts, and Delaware.

In a similar way, proximity to the Atlantic has influenced everything from the region's architecture (weathered shingles and captain's walks) to its settlement patterns (note the bustling port towns) to its folklore (such as shipwreck stories and sea chanteys). For coastal dwellers, the ocean is not just part of the scenery: it's an active player in community life. It delivers welcome breezes and destructive storms. It creates sweet sandy beaches and then sweeps them back to sea. Most significant, it sets a tidal tempo by which many human communities—and all nearby ecological communities—organize their lives.

Habitats

Every wild creature that lives along the North Atlantic Coast is adapted in some way to conditions created by the sea. But not all species can tolerate the same conditions. The particular type of place where a creature finds the food, shelter, and space it needs to thrive is called its *habitat*. Not surprisingly, there are many different habitats along this northern coast—from small suburban backyards to the vast expanse of the open ocean. The following sections highlight some of the dominant wildlife habitats of this region and describe some of the plants and animals that live there.

Rocky Shores: Rocky shores dominate the North Atlantic Coast, especially from Canada to Maine. Over very long periods of time, the action of waves will weather these rocks into sandy beaches. For now, they offer dramatic views and a chance to witness the stratified strategy of rock-dwelling sea life.

If you visit the rocky shore during low tide, you may be able to pick out some of the different zones of life stretching from land to sea. High on the rocks is the *periwinkle zone,* an area submerged only during the very highest tides. Periwinkles are small sea snails. They may appear to be rooted in place, but in fact, they inch up and down the rock in response to the monthly high and low tides. Between the high-tide and low-tide mark lies the *barnacle zone,* where rock or acorn barnacles become most abundant. These are tough creatures who put up with pounding surf, predators, and winter ice. When you see them exposed to the air, their shells will usually be tightly closed. But when submerged, they open up like great hungry mouths and sweep in tiny plants and animals from the water. Below these barnacles and the low-tide line lies the *kelp zone*. Here long, strong kelp plants hold fast to the rocks against the constant push and pull of the waves. Around their base live a pack of other creatures, including mussels, spiny sea urchins, and oysters.

One other great place for viewing coastal creatures along rocky shores is in *tide pools*—shallow ponds left between the rocks at low tide. Size and location tend to determine who resides within a particular tide pool. You might see colorful starfish or sea anemones clinging to the rocks or catch a glimpse of rockpool shrimps darting through the water. (Examples: "New Hampshire Shore: Haiku"; "The Fog Maiden's Necklace.")

Sandy Beaches and Dunes: Visit a beach, and your first impression may be of a broad blank canvas: blue sky, blue waters, and tawny sand. Gulls and sunbathers may seem to be the only visible forms of life. But look again. Stand ankle deep, and you may be able to spot sand dollars, sea cucumbers, or other sun-sensitive organisms nestled in the sand beneath your feet. Then look at the surface of the water and you should be able to see bits of debris being tossed to the shore. That's the ocean's smorgasbord—bits of kelp and fish particles and tiny plants and animals—delivered wave after wave to the wet sand. Burrowed beneath your toes are worms that eat the sand and shellfish that suck in water to get to these nutritious morsels. If you can't find any of these burrowers, try looking for their holes. Or, look for shorebirds along the water's edge. Some skitter to and fro with the waves, dipping in the water for their meal. Others patrol the high-tide mark for the tasty jetsam left there.

Now head up the beach. Soon you'll reach the foredune—a hump of sand anchored by hardy beach grass. There's not much life here—the conditions are too windy and too dry. But just over the dune lie sheltered hollows where beach plum, beach heather, and bayberry take hold. Some of these hollows are even moist enough to harbor wild cranberries and other bog plants. Continue on and you may find miniature forests of cedar and pitch pine. Salty winds kill most of these trees' new growth, so they stay stunted. But they offer enough protection for rabbits, mice, songbirds, and more.

Come back at night to see more beach wildlife: ghost crabs creeping along the water's edge and shrimplike sandhoppers popping up from the sand. (Examples: "Of Beaches, Bays, and My Boyhood with the Colonel"; "Fledgling Summer"; "Fire Island Walking Song.")

Tidal Flats: Twice a day, the receding tide reveals sandy or muddy flats along many parts of the North Atlantic Coast. During the lowest tides of the month, the flats are at their most exposed. That's your best chance for seeing clams and other tidal inhabitants. But it won't be easy. All residents of the flats must endure the alternating extremes of flooding and complete exposure. Burrowing underground is usually their best way of avoiding sun and predators, such as black-bellied plovers, green crabs, and gulls. Some, like the razor clam, are such speedy diggers that you probably wouldn't even be able to catch one if you dug after it! (Examples: "The Magic of the Flats"; "Where the River Meets the Sea.")

Rivers and Lakes: Freshwater rivers and lakes along the North Atlantic are home to many creatures you won't find right at the seashore. Willows may grow along the shore, and trout and pickerel may meander

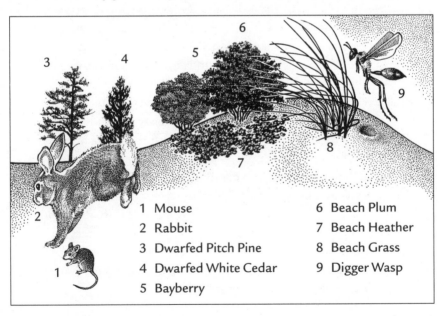

1 Mouse
2 Rabbit
3 Dwarfed Pitch Pine
4 Dwarfed White Cedar
5 Bayberry
6 Beach Plum
7 Beach Heather
8 Beach Grass
9 Digger Wasp

through the water. But you can still spot some ocean influences on many freshwater rivers in this region. For example, some coastal rivers rise and fall dramatically with the tides. And some boast saltwater fish—such as alewives and shad—that migrate between the ocean and inland water bodies at different points in their lives. Many fish also begin their lives in *estuaries*, which form the transition zone between these freshwater and saltwater environments. (Examples: "Never Go Home without a Fish"; "The Legend of the Mashpee Maiden.")

Salt Marshes: Just as people are attracted to a well-stocked kitchen, so are coastal organisms drawn to the nutrient-rich waters of the salt marsh. Here the tides deliver a regular supply of nutrients, which get trapped by salt-marsh grasses. As salt-marsh plants and animals grow, die, and decay, they add even more nutrients to the mud or sand below. If you visit a salt marsh, you're likely to spot some of the beneficiaries of this ample food supply. Snails cling to the cordgrass. Muskrats crawl along the ground, building domed lodges to protect themselves and their young. Herons and bitterns stand still among the reeds, while redwinged blackbirds, sparrows, and marsh wrens swoop overhead.

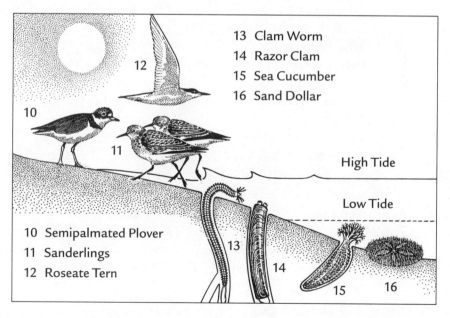

13 Clam Worm
14 Razor Clam
15 Sea Cucumber
16 Sand Dollar

High Tide

Low Tide

10 Semipalmated Plover
11 Sanderlings
12 Roseate Tern

You'll find salt marshes all along the North Atlantic Coast, where their presence is a blessing in all sorts of ways. Salt marshes provide a buffer against storm waves. They help purify coastal waters. They are twice as productive as most of our farms, producing food for hundreds of thousands of migrating waterfowl and countless other critters. And they're nursery grounds, where young ducklings, fiddler crabs, mussels, and many other creatures begin their lives. (Example: "The Great Marsh.")

Heathlands and Grasslands: Climb up the shore in certain parts of the North Atlantic Coast, and you may come across a heathland—an open meadow filled with low shrubs and wildflowers. The plants that live here are hardy: they can grow where the soil is poor and the air is laced with salt from the sea. If you visit the heathlands of Maine during the summer months, you may be in for a treat: wild blueberries! Heathlands are also the favored habitat of some rare bird species, including the short-eared owl.

Similar, but more rare, are the North Atlantic Coast's grasslands. Found in such places as Long Island, Nantucket, and Martha's Vineyard, these areas are like a pocket of prairie right next to the sea! In fact, some of these grasslands were once home to the heath hen, the East Coast's version of the prairie chicken. Today, ecologists are working to restore grasslands along the North Atlantic Coast. They won't be able to bring back the heath hen, but they can help other species that thrive in these grasslands, including the rare grasshopper sparrow. (Example: "Blueberries.")

Forests: While dwarfed forests of cedar, pitch pine, holly, and sassafras may be the norm near the dunes, tall trees are not absent from the North Atlantic Coast. In fact, impressive forests of spruce and fir still grow near the shore in parts of Canada and Maine. Farther south, oaks and hickories have sprouted on many of the lands that used to be farms. And pine-oak woodlands dominate the sandy, less fertile soils of this region. (Examples: "Otter Delight"; "A White Heron.")

Urban Parks: Even if you live in the city, you can see some of the North Atlantic's wildlife in nearby parks or even in a backyard tree! Many birds stop in city parks during fall and spring migrations. For example, New York City's Central Park is a haven for migrating warblers. Other creatures have been able to adapt to the urban environment. Raccoons and opossums feed on our scraps and trash. Peregrine falcons dive-bomb pigeons in the valleys between skyscrapers, much as they once caught prey between vertical cliffs. Gray squirrels, robins, and even red-tailed hawks have proven resilient to much of the hustle and bustle of urban life. But of course, the more we keep our urban lands and waterways safe, clean, and undisturbed, the better chance we'll have of keeping these and other creatures as our neighbors. (Examples: "Roostwatch"; "A Moth Flies in Brooklyn.")

Animals and Plants

It would take a whole book to describe the animals and plants of the North Atlantic Coast. So, we've simply listed below the organisms mentioned in this anthology and given a brief explanation, where necessary, of what they are.

Ruddy Turnstone

Birds: Birds fall into several big categories, which may help to keep them straight. The *swimmers,* such as mallards, loons, and Canada geese, stick close to the water. The *aerialists,* or flyers, are seabirds such as laughing gulls, herring gulls (which are sometimes called seagulls), black skimmers, and terns (including roseate terns and common terns). *Long-legged wading birds,* frequently found in marshes, include bitterns, great blue herons, green herons, and snowy egrets. Many *smaller wading birds* feed close to the ocean's edge. These include piping plovers, red knots, ruddy turnstones, sandpipers, and killdeer. Pheasants are an example of *fowl-like birds.* Hawks, ospreys, eagles, owls, and merlins (which are small falcons) are all *birds of prey,* or raptors. They have talons, sharp beaks, and terrific eyesight, helping them catch small rodents and other prey. *Perching birds* make up a large category that includes red-winged blackbirds, ravens, sparrows, crows, wrens, indigo buntings, warblers, golden-crowned kinglets, cedar waxwings, chickadees, starlings, pigeons, cardinals, scarlet tanagers, rose-breasted

Golden-Crowned Kinglet

Merlin

grosbeaks, orchard orioles, yellow-billed cuckoos, least flycatchers, great crested flycatchers, wood thrushes, blue jays, titmice, robins, and mockingbirds. And finally, the *non-perching land birds* are kingfishers; downy, red-bellied, and hairy woodpeckers; flickers and yellow-bellied sapsuckers (which are woodpeckers, too); phoebes; and whippoorwills.

Fin Whale

Mammals:

Many people don't realize it, but dolphins, porpoises, and whales—including humpbacks, fins, sulphurs, potheads, and, biggest of all, the blue whale—are marine mammals. Some of the mammals living near the seashore include beavers, mink, muskrats, otters, and raccoons. And the mammals of nearby parks and woodlands include squirrels, foxes, bears, white-footed mice, voles (another kind of rodent), chipmunks, rats, bats, and deer.

Marine Invertebrates: Marine invertebrates are sea creatures that don't have a backbone. You can group them in the following way. *Jellylike animals* include jellyfish and sea anemones. *Mollusks* include coffee-bean snails, whelks, conchs, augers, sundials, limpets, and periwinkles, as well as all the bivalves, or two-shelled organisms: clams, oysters, scallops, mussels, soft-shelled clams, razor clams, and quahogs.

Lobster

Knobbed Whelk

(Quahogs are called cherrystone clams when they're at their smallest, littlenecks when they're a bit bigger, and quahogs when they're full grown.) Lobsters, barnacles, fiddler crabs, hermit crabs, ghost crabs, mud crabs, sandhoppers (or beach fleas), and shrimp are all crustaceans, and they're in the same broader group as horseshoe crabs: the *arthropods*. The spiny skinned *echinoderms* include sea stars (or starfish), sea urchins, sea cucumbers, and sand dollars.

Freshwater and Terrestrial Invertebrates: Crayfish are freshwater invertebrates. Terrestrial invertebrates (those that live on land) include wolf spiders and other spiders, and *insects,* such as crickets, powdered butterflies, *cynthia* moths, mayflies, grasshoppers, bees, beetles, ants, chinch (or cinch) bugs, plant hoppers, and, of course, mosquitoes.

Reptiles and Amphibians: Painted turtles and diamondback terrapins are *reptiles.* That means they have claws on their feet and their skin is dry and scaly, and they lay their eggs on land. Salamanders, frogs, and toads are all *amphibians.* Clawless with moist skin, they lay their eggs in the water, and their young go through a change called metamorphosis as they develop into adulthood.

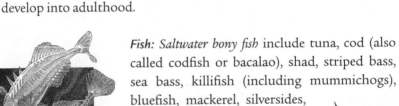

Diamondback Terrapin

Fish: Saltwater bony fish include tuna, cod (also called codfish or bacalao), shad, striped bass, sea bass, killifish (including mummichogs), bluefish, mackerel, silversides, sticklebacks, northern pipefish, eels, white perch, herrings, anchovies, menhadens, searobins, naked gobies, striped mullets, croackers, northern kingfish, flounders, and flukes. A "mermaid's purse" is the egg sac of a saltwater fish called a skate. *Freshwater bony fish*

Four-Spined Stickleback

Mermaid's Purse

include minnows, hornpouts, yellow perch, smallmouth bass, pickerel, salmon, and trout. (Some of the fish listed above spend portions of their lives in both fresh and saltwater environments.) Finally, sharks are in a category all their own: they're *cartilaginous fish*.

Plants: These are the *tall, broadleaf trees* mentioned in the readings: maple, oak, hickory, elm, magnolia, American chestnut, willow, poplar, black cherry, beech, linden, paper birch, walnut, holly, London planetree (a relative of the sycamore), and ailanthus (also known as tree-of-heaven). The *coniferous trees* include cedar, spruce, hemlock, and pine trees. *Smaller broadleaf shrubs* include rhododendron, low and high bush blueberry, cranberry, and bayberry. The following are, broadly speaking, *wildflowers:* dandelion, lady slipper, rose, cattail, aster, gayfeather, lily of the valley, plantain, milkweed, sunflower, purple bee balm, groundnut, wake-robin, marigold, daisy, Solomon's seal, partridgeberry, strawberry, huckleberry, goldenrod, rushes, cordgrass, beach grass, beach heather, sea myrtle, and knotweed.

Blueberries

Not all the plants mentioned in the readings are native to the North Atlantic Coast. For example, ailanthus, dandelions, sunflowers, marigolds, and daisies come from other regions (or continents) but have become common in this region over time.

Other: Mushrooms are a kind of *fungus*. Neither fungi, nor the group of organisms called *algae* are now considered part of the plant family. Algae range from tiny, single-celled organisms to large seaweeds, such as kelp. Sea lettuce is also a kind of algae. *Lichens* are made up of fungi living symbiotically with colonies of microscopic algae.

Stories by State
or Province

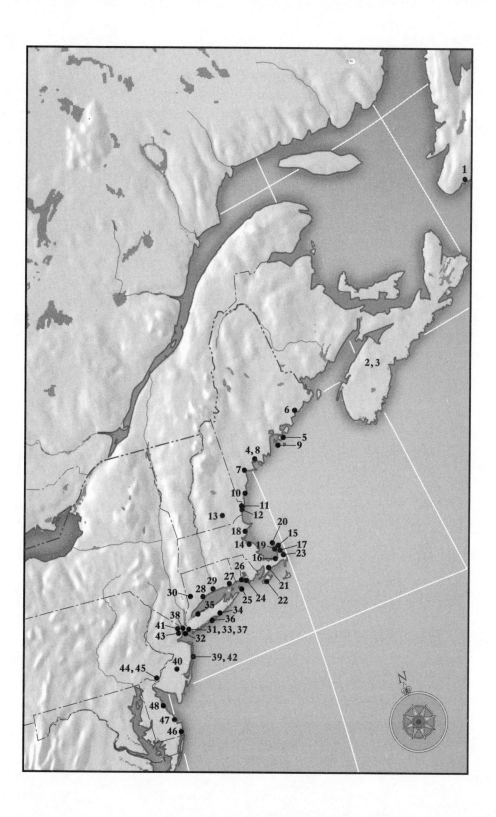

Parks and Preserves

Listed below are just a few of the many places where you can go to experience the wilder side of the North Atlantic Coast region. Please note: the phone numbers provided are sometimes for the park's headquarters, but often for a managing agency or organization. In any case, the people at these numbers can provide you with details about the area and directions for how to get there!

Connecticut

Audubon Center in Greenwich (Greenwich) 203-869-5272
Bluff Point State Park (Groton) 860-424-3200
Connecticut Audubon Center at Fairfield (Fairfield) 203-259-6305
Hammonasset Beach State Park (Madison) 203-245-2785
Lighthouse Point Park (New Haven) 203-946-8005
Stuart B. McKinney National Wildlife Refuge (Westbrook)
   860-399-2513
Milford Point Bird Sanctuary (Milford) 203-878-7440

Delaware

Brandywine Creek State Park (Wilmington) 302-577-3534
Bombay Hook National Wildlife Refuge (Smyrna) 302-653-9345
Cape Henlopen State Parks (Lewes) 302-645-8983
Delaware Seashore State Park (Rehoboth Beach) 302-227-2800
Robert L. Graham/Nanticoke Wildlife Area (Laurel) 302-739-5297
Great Cypress Swamp (Selbyville) 302-653-2880
Killens Pond State Park (Felton) 302-284-4526
Little Creek Wildlife Area (Little Creek) 302-739-5297
Lums Pond State Park (Bear) 302-368-6989

Pea Patch Island (Delaware City) 302-834-7941
Prime Hook National Wildlife Refuge (Milton) 302-684-8419
Trap Pond State Park (Laurel) 302-875-5153
Norman G. Wilder Wildlife Area (Viola) 302-739-5297

Maine

Acadia National Park (Bar Harbor) 207-288-3338
Back Cove (Portland) 207-772-4994
Biddeford Pool/East Point Sanctuary (Biddeford) 207-781-2330
Cobscook Bay State Park (Dennysville) 207-726-4412
Gilsland Farm (Falmouth) 207-781-2330
Great Wass Island Preserve (Beals) 207-729-5181
Indian Point-Blagden Preserve (Bar Harbor) 207-729-5181
Machias Seal Island (contact boat companies in Jonesport:
    207-497-5933; Lubec: 207-733-5584; or Cutler: 207-259-4484)
Matinicus Island and Matinicus Rock (Matinicus) 207-366-3868
Monhegan Island (contact boat companies in Port Clyde:
    207-372-8848; Boothbay Harbor: 800-298-2284; or New Harbor:
    207-677-2026)
Petit Manan National Wildlife Refuge (Milbridge) 207-546-2124
Quoddy Head State Park (Lubec) 207-733-0911
Rachel Carson National Wildlife Refuge (Wells) 207-646-9226
Rachel Carson Salt Pond Preserve (New Harbor) 207-729-5181
Roque Bluffs State Park (Roque Bluffs) 207-255-3475
Scarborough Marsh (Scarborough) 207-781-2330
Wells National Estuarine Research Reserve (Wells) 207-646-1555
Wolfe's Neck Woods State Park (Freeport) 207-624-6080 (Nov.–Mar.)
    and 207-865-4465 (Apr.–Oct.)

Massachusetts

Blue Hills Reservation (Milton) 617-698-1802
Cape Cod National Seashore (extensive region on Cape Cod)
    508-255-3421
Daniel Webster Wildlife Sanctuary (Marshfield) 781-837-9400
Demarest Lloyd State Park (Dartmouth) 508-636-3298

Eastern Point Wildlife Sanctuary (Gloucester) 781-259-9500

Great Meadows National Wildlife Refuge (Sudbury and Concord) 978-443-4661

Halibut Point State Park (Rockport) 978-546-2997

Marblehead Neck Wildlife Sanctuary (Marblehead) 978-887-9264

Martha's Vineyard (contact Chamber of Commerce: 508-693-0085 or Mass. Audubon Society: 508-627-4850)

Middlesex Fells Reservation (Stoneham) 617-727-5215

Monomoy National Wildlife Refuge (Chatham) 508-945-0594

Mount Auburn Cemetery (Cambridge) 617-547-7105

Nantucket Island (contact Chamber of Commerce: 508-228-1700 or Maria Mitchell Assoc.: 508-228-9198)

Parker River National Wildlife Refuge/Plum Island (Newburyport) 978-465-5753

Plymouth Beach (Plymouth) 800-872-1620

Wellfleet Bay Wildlife Sanctuary (South Wellfleet) 508-349-2615

New Hampshire

Beaver Brook Association (Milford, Brookline, Hollis) 603-465-7787

Isle of Shoals (contact boat company: 603-431-5500 or 800-441-4620; or Audubon Society of N.H.: 603-224-9909)

Odiorne Point State Park (Rye) 603-436-8043

New Jersey

Bennett Bogs Preserve (Lower Township, Cape May County) 908-879-7262

Cape May Point State Park (Cape May Point) 609-884-2159

Edwin B. Forsythe National Wildlife Refuge, Brigantine Division (Oceanville) 609-652-1665

Gateway National Recreation Area, Sandy Hook Unit (Highlands) 732-872-5970

Great Bay Wildlife Management Area (Tuckertown) 609-259-2132

Great Swamp National Wildlife Refuge (Basking Ridge) 973-425-1222

Kearny Marsh (Kearny) 201-460-1700

McNamara Wildlife Management Area (Marmora) 609-292-2965

Parvin State Park (Vineland) 609-358-8616
Reed's Beach (Dennisville) 609-628-2103
Webb's Mill Bog (Whiting) 609-292-2965
Wharton State Forest (Batsto) 609-561-0024

New York

Central Park (New York City) 212-360-3444
Fire Island National Seashore (Patchogue) 516-289-4810
Gateway National Recreation Area, Jamaica Bay Unit (New York City-
    Queens) 718-318-4340
Long Pond Greenbelt (Sag Harbor) 516-367-3225
Montauk Point State Park (Montauk) 516-668-3781

Rhode Island

Beavertail State Park (Jamestown) 401-884-2010
Block Island (contact Chamber of Commerce: 401-466-2982)
Brenton Point State Park (Newport) 401-847-2400
Burlingame State Park (Charlestown) 401-322-7337
Great Swamp Wildlife Management Area (West Kingston)
    401-789-0281
Ninigret National Wildlife Refuge (Charlestown) 401-364-9124
Norman Bird Sanctuary (Middletown) 401-846-2577
George B. Parker Woodland (Coventry and Foster) 401-949-5454
Sachuest Point National Wildlife Refuge (Middletown) 401-847-5511
Sakonnet Point (Little Compton) 401-789-0281
Swan Point Cemetery (Providence) 401-272-1314
Trustom Pond National Wildlife Refuge (South Kingston)
    401-364-9124

Recommended Reading

Alden, Peter and Brian Cassie, et al. *The National Audubon Society Field Guide to the Mid-Atlantic States.* New York: Alfred A. Knopf, 1999.

Alden, Peter and Brian Cassie, et al. *The National Audubon Society Field Guide to New England.* New York: Alfred A. Knopf, 1998.

Amos, William H. *The Life of the Seashore.* New York: McGraw-Hill Book Company, 1966.

Bredeson, Carmen. *Tide Pools.* Danbury, Conn.: Franklin Watts, 1999.

Finch, Robert. *Smithsonian Guide to Natural America: Southern New England.* Washington D.C.: Smithsonian Books and New York: Random House, Inc., 1996.

Gosner, Kenneth L. and Roger Tory Peterson. *A Field Guide to the Atlantic Seashore.* Boston: Houghton Mifflin, 1999.

Hay, John and Peter Farb. *The Atlantic Shore: Human and Natural History from Long Island to Labrador.* New York: Harper and Row, 1966.

Kochanoff, Peggy. *Beachcombing the Atlantic Coast.* Missoula, Mont.: Mountain Press, 1997.

Martinez, Andrew J. *Marine Life of the North Atlantic: Canada to New England.* Camden, Maine: Down East Books, 1999.

Teal, John and Mildred. *Life and Death of the Salt Marsh.* New York: Ballatine Books, 1971.

Special Thanks

Seven years ago, in the inspiring company of Mount Abraham and a gaggle of nature writers, I happened upon the first ideas for this book. Since then, more people than I can name have helped me turn these ideas into the reality of a children's literary series. I hope the following list, however incomplete, helps to express my gratitude for this assistance.

First, a thanks to John Elder, Gary Paul Nabhan, Richard Nelson, Terry Tempest Williams, Chris Merrill, Laurie Lane-Zucker, and Jennifer Sahn for the thoughtful and ebullient company that so inspired me on that bright autumn weekend. Soon after, Olivia Gilliam listened and shared her gentle insights, and she left us too soon.

With heartfelt gratitude I thank the echoing green foundation for supporting my early work on this project, and for believing in young people's big, tenacious dreams. The echoing green community gave me practical guidance, and, most important, some lifelong friends.

Three cheers go to some of the teachers who are working to bring kids back in touch with the natural world, and who helped me test early curriculum ideas: Juanita Lavadie and Randy Thorne of Taos Pueblo School; Lynn Grimes of Turquoise Trail School in Santa Fe; Jen Fong, formerly of Bronx Green-Up; Karen Rogers Childress of Rural Resources in Greenville, Tennessee; and Alex Glass and Wyatt Weber of Watkins Elementary School in Washington, D.C.

When it came time to create this first anthology, several colleagues and friends offered expertise and assistance. Great thanks to Miriam Stewart and Robin Kelsey, perceptive readers; to E. Barrie Kavasch for reviewing our Lenape story; to Bruce Hammond of The Nature Conservancy for helping me get my ecological facts straight; to Jen Kretser and Priscilla Howell for inspired and enthusiastic feedback on the book's content and format; and to the many friends who shared with me their favorite North Atlantic literature.

Finally, deepest thanks go to the staff of Milkweed Editions, for undertaking and guiding this project; to Gary Paul Nabhan, for wise counsel and enduring faith; and to my best friend and best husband, Robin, for all things great and small.

Contributor Acknowledgments

Jennifer Ackerman, "The Great Marsh," excerpted from *Notes from the Shore* (New York: Viking Penguin, 1995), 114–15, 118–21. Copyright © 1995 by Jennifer Ackerman. Reprinted with permission from Viking Penguin, a division of Penguin Putnam Inc.

Nadya Aisenberg, "Today." Copyright © 2000 by Nadya Aisenberg. Printed with permission from the author.

Jeff W. Bens, "The Legend of Big Claw." Copyright © 2000 by Jeff W. Bens. Printed with permission from the author.

Henry Beston, "Stranded," excerpted from *The Outermost House* (New York: Rinehart & Company, 1928), 78–80. Copyright © 1928, 1949, 1956 by Henry Beston, © 1977 by Elizabeth C. Beston. Reprinted with permission from Henry Holt and Company, LLC.

Alice Stone Blackwell, "Dorchester Days," excerpted from *Growing Up in Boston's Gilded Age: The Journal of Alice Stone Blackwell, 1872–1874,* ed. Marlene Deahl Merrill (New Haven, Conn.: Yale University Press, 1990), 49, 66, 91, 109, 112–113, 162, 163, 169, 176, 177, 188. Copyright © 1990 by Yale University. Reprinted with permission from Yale University Press.

Mélina Brown, "Cranberry Cove." Copyright © 2000 by Mélina Brown. Printed with permission from the author.

Joseph Bruchac, "Glooskap and the Whale," in *Return of the Sun* (Freedom, Calif.: Crossing Press, 1990), 73–76. Copyright © 1990 by Joseph Bruchac. Reprinted with permission from The Crossing Press, P.O. Box 1048, Freedom, CA 95019.

Tyler Cadman, "Golden-Crowned Kinglet," in *River of Words: The Natural World as Viewed by Young People,* ed. Robert Hass (Berkeley, Calif.: River of Words, 1999), 11. Copyright © 1999 from River of Words. Reprinted with permission from River of Words Poetry and Art Contest.

Sarah Orne Jewett, "A White Heron," in *The Country of the Pointed Firs and Other Stories* (Garden City, N.Y.: Doubleday, 1956), 161–71.

Rita Joe, "Aye! no monuments," in *Poems of Rita Joe* (Sydney, Nova Scotia: Abanaki Press, 1979), 10. Copyright © 1979 by Rita Joe. Reprinted with permission from the author.

Helen Keller, "A Summer in Brewster," excerpted from *The Story of My Life* (Garden City, N.Y.: Doubleday, 1954), 51–52.

Eugene F. Kinkead, "Fire Island Walking Song," in the *New Yorker* 33, no. 28 (August 31, 1957): 51. Copyright © 1957 by Eugene F. Kinkead. Reprinted with permission from the *New Yorker*. All rights reserved.

Norbert Krapf, "Long Island Crow," in *Arriving on Paumanok* (Port Jefferson, N.Y.: Street Press, 1979), 8. Copyright © 1979 by Norbert Krapf. Reprinted with permission from the author.

Virginia Kroll, "Lunch with a Gull," in *Story Friends* 94, no. 7 (July 1999): 16. Copyright © 1999 by Virginia Kroll. Reprinted with permission from the author.

Adrian Kingsbury Lane, "Log of the *Downit*," excerpted from *Log of the Downit*, ed. Richard Knowles Morris (Noank, Conn.: Noank Historical Society, 1993), 4, 5, 8, 15, 16, 17, 22. Copyright © 1995 by Highlights for Children, Inc. Reprinted with permission from Highlights for Children, Inc., Columbus, Ohio.

Clare Leighton, "The Magic of the Flats," excerpted from *Where Land Meets Sea* (New York: Rinehart and Company, 1954), 41–42, 43–47, 50–53, 55. Copyright © 1954 by Clare Leighton. Reprinted with permission from Devin-Adair, Publishers, Inc., Old Greenwich, CT 06870. All rights reserved.

April Lindner, "Seascape." Copyright © 2000 by April Lindner. Printed with permission from the author.

Diane Mayr, "New Hampshire Shore: Haiku." Copyright © 2000 by Diane Mayr. Printed with permission from the author.

Cecile Mazzucco-Than, "Three Trees in the City." Copyright © 2000 by Cecile Mazzucco-Than. Printed with permission from the author.

Farley Mowat, "The Great Whale," excerpted from *A Whale for the Killing* (Boston: Little, Brown and Company, 1972), 124–29. Copyright © 1972 by Farley Mowat Limited. Reprinted with permission from Little, Brown and Company, Inc. and McClelland & Stewart, Inc., *The Canadian Publishers*.

Mary Oliver, "Starfish," in *Dream Work* (New York: Atlantic Monthly Press, 1986), 36–37. Copyright © 1986 by Mary Oliver. Reprinted with permission from the author.

Julie Parson-Nesbitt, "Pauline Sings across the Rooftops." Copyright © 2000 by Julie Parson-Nesbitt. Printed with permission from the author.

Mary Quigley, "The Ocean Is a Heartbeat." Copyright © 2000 by Mary Quigley. Printed with permission from the author.

Elizabeth Reynard, "The Legend of the Mashpee Maiden," in *The Narrow Land* (Cambridge, Mass.: Riverside Press, 1934), 31–33. Copyright © 1934 by Elizabeth Reynard. Reprinted with permission from the Chatham Historical Society, Chatham, Massachusetts.

Elisavietta Ritchie, "Persistent Haiku." Copyright © 2000 by Elisavietta Ritchie. Reprinted with permission from the author. Originally published in *Christian Science Monitor.*

Marybeth Rua-Larsen, "Pickering Beach." Copyright © 2000 by Marybeth Rua-Larsen. Printed with permission from the author.

David Sobel, "Otter Delight," in *Sanctuary: The Journal of the Massachusetts Audubon Society* 21, no. 5 (January 1982): 7–8. Copyright © 1982 by David Sobel. Reprinted with permission from the author.

Anne Spollen, "Of the Sea." Copyright © 2000 by Anne Spollen. Printed with permission from the author.

Jennifer Stansbury, "Fledgling Summer." Copyright © 2000 by Jennifer Stansbury. Printed with permission from the author.

Wally Swist, "Shells," in *The New Life* (West Hartford, Conn.: Plinth Books, 1998), 65. Copyright © 1998 by Wally Swist. Reprinted with permission from the author.

Henry David Thoreau, "A Wild, Rank Place," excerpted from *Cape Cod* (New York: Thomas Y. Crowell Company, 1961), 214–16.

William W. Warner, "Of Beaches, Bays, and My Boyhood with the Colonel," in *Heart of the Land: Essays on Last Great Places*, ed. Joseph Barbato and Lisa Weinerman (New York: Pantheon Books, 1994), 60–64. Copyright © 1994 by William W. Warner. Reprinted with permission from the author. Republished as "A Prologue, by the Sea," in *Into the Porcupine Cave and Other Odysseys: Adventures of an Occasional Naturalist* (Washington, D.C.: National Geographic Society, 1999).

Marie Winn, "Roostwatch," in *Red-Tails in Love* (New York: Pantheon Books, 1998), 153–61. Copyright © 1998 by Marie Winn. Reprinted with permission from Pantheon Books, a division of Random House, Inc.

About the Editor

Sara St. Antoine grew up in Ann Arbor, Michigan. She holds a bachelor's degree in English from Williams College and a master's degree in Environmental Studies from the Yale School of Forestry and Environmental Studies. Currently living in Cambridge, Massachusetts, she enjoys walking along the Charles River and seeing black-crowned night herons hunkered in the trees.

About the Illustrators

Paul Mirocha is a designer and illustrator of books about nature for children and adults. His first book, *Gathering the Desert*, by Gary Paul Nabhan, won the 1985 John Burroughs Medal for natural history. He lives in Tucson, Arizona, with his daughters, Anna and Claire.

Trudy Nicholson is an illustrator of nature with a background in medical and scientific illustration. She received her B.S. in Fine Arts at Columbia University and has worked as a natural-science illustrator in a variety of scientific fields for many years. She lives in Maryland.

The World As Home

The World As Home, a publishing program of Milkweed Editions, is dedicated to exploring and expanding our relationship with the natural world. These books are a forum for distinctive writing that alerts the reader to vital issues and offers personal testimonies to living harmoniously with the world around us. Learn more about the World As Home at www.milkweed.org/worldashome.

Milkweed Editions

Founded in 1979, Milkweed Editions is the largest independent, nonprofit, literary publisher in the United States. Milkweed publishes with the intention of making a humane impact on society, in the belief that good writing can transform the human heart and spirit. Within this mission, Milkweed publishes in five areas: fiction, nonfiction, poetry, children's literature for middle-grade readers, and the World As Home.

Join Us

Along with the sales of its books, Milkweed depends on the generosity of foundations and individuals like you. In an increasingly consolidated and bottom-line driven publishing, your support allows us to select and publish books on the basis of their literary quality and the depth of their message. Please visit our Web site, www.milkweed.org, or contact us at 800-520-6455 to learn more about our donor program.

Interior design by Wendy Holdman.
The text is typeset in 12/16 point Legacy Book
by Stanton Publication Services, Inc.
Printed on acid-free 50# Fraser Trade Book paper
by Friesen Corporation.